Soulmates

Don DeBon

Soulmates

Don DeBon

First Printing
Copyright © 2014 Don DeBon

ISBN 978-0-9881783-4-2
ISBN 978-0-9881783-3-5 (**e-book**)

Dedicated to the one special woman in my life who convinced me to take up my pen again.

Not to mention my wonderful editors. This book would not have been possible without you.

Contents

Pain tiptoed though her mind as Aleshia pulled the pillow over her head to block the sunlight pouring though the window. It helped, but her head still ached. "Not again. To feel like this, I should have had too much fun last night," she muttered beneath the pillow as Miles entered. Roughly human shaped but with a large dome instead of a standard type head, Miles was one of the nicer of the Mechand models allowed for home use. He did many of the duties no one else wanted: cooking, cleaning, and making sure the refrigerator was stocked. He could be further enhanced, but Aleshia liked to do many things herself. As usual, Miles had activated his anti-grav, allowing him to float a few inches off the ground and enter quietly. "Miss Aleshia, it is time to get up." He said in his gentle, yet artificial voice.

"Ugh! Can I sleep a little more? Or at least try to?" Her words were muffled though the pillow, but not beyond Miles' recognition abilities.

"I am sorry, but you did ask me to wake you at this time. You do have that important appointment today, if you recall."

Aleshia popped up from under the pillow pushing the dull ache away for the moment. "Oh it is Tuesday isn't it? I forgot

I am meeting Mindy today. What time is it?"

"9:00am standard, your appointment is at 11:00am standard. I estimate you have enough time to ready yourself and transport there if you begin now."

Aleshia sat up and stretched. "Sometimes you take all the fun out of it, Miles."

"The fun out of what?" Miles asked still hovering by her bed.

"Never mind. I had better get ready. Mindy will be wondering if I am late. We have been looking forward to this shopping trip for quite a while."

"I do not understand why you wish to go shopping for clothing when I can create anything you might require."

"Miles, it is a girl thing. You wouldn't understand."

"A girl thing? Yes it is apparently beyond my understanding why someone would want to travel to a store halfway around the planet for items that were created using the same basic templates I have and require less expended energy to complete."

"Miles, just go make breakfast and I will be down in a few minutes."

"Yes Miss Aleshia." Miles said as he inclined his dome, then hovered out of the room.

Aleshia crawled out of bed and drug herself to the sonic shower. This morning though, the sonic didn't feel potent enough. She keyed in her code to use a ration of actual water and the jet turned on bathing her in luxurious liquid. She relished in its warm embrace for several extra minutes before turning it off and climbing out. The shower had helped push the headache back into the invisible box from where it came. She dried herself off and placed the towel in the cleaning drawer and set it to auto. Walking over to her closet, she found the dress she wanted to wear today. A strapless design with a short skirt that came to her mid thigh. Just enough to make things interesting, should she find someone to be interesting with. She then put on a pair of adjustable pumps and set the height to two inches, and the color to match the emerald dress she now wore.

Walking downstairs she found Miles had finished breakfast, and her usual place was already set. She sat down as her nose caught the wonderful scents wafting through the air. "Mmmm it smells good."

"It is your usual, synth egg, bacon, and waffles. Supplies are running low. I need to refill them in the next few days. Do you authorize me to procure more with your normal rations?"

"Yes Miles," she said while munching on the strip of bacon, "that is fine. How much will you need?"

"No more than a third of your total for the month, but I shouldn't need to acquire any more for some time."

Aleshia nodded. "That won't be a problem, I can apply for more if we need. I doubt it will be necessary though, the ration has always lasted before."

"Yes I concur, I do not believe you will exhaust the existing ration. And even then you have quite a bit on your reserve that you have accumulated from past unused totals."

"Exactly. I think ..." She dropped the fork and held her head as a sudden searing pain raced through her mind. It felt like someone was drilling into her brain with a dull razor. Almost as quickly as it began, the pain lessened and disappeared.

"Miss Aleshia? Are you all right?" Miles said as he hovered over to her.

"Yes I'm fine Miles. Thank you."

"I beg to differ. Your actions indicate another headache,

correct? That makes three this past week. May I call a med-tech this time?"

"NO! I am fine. You are not to call or notify anyone, is that clear?"

"Acknowledged," Miles said as he craned his head dome a little in Aleshia's direction, "but I really think I should call a med-tech or at least let me scan you."

"NO DOCTORS! And I do not want you scanning me either, is that clear?"

"Yes, perfectly clear."

"Good," Aleshia said as she got up from the table, "make sure you get more of that chocolate cream cake I like. We haven't had it in a long time."

"I will try, but you know that the raw materials are more resource consuming. I may not be able to with the current budget."

Aleshia waved her hand dismissively. "Just get it. I have enough back ration credits to pay for it. I can afford to treat myself once in a while."

"Acknowledged. Will there be anything else Miss Aleshia?" Miles said as he took the dirty plate, silverware, and hovered over to the sink to begin the cleaning process.

"Nope. That's all. Thanks Miles."

"You are welcome Miss Aleshia. And if I may make an inquiry, why are you wearing the impractical shoes today?"

Aleshia laughed. "Because they make my legs look good. And I am going out today."

"But you could damage yourself with such footwear." Miles said as he finished cleaning and sterilizing the dishes.

Aleshia laughed again. "You worry too much. Look these are adjustable, if I have problems I can always lower the heel. All right?"

"I suppose. However, I do not understand the reason behind them. If you are trying to attract a mate, it would be far easier to file with the central systems that you want one. I am sure with all of your attributes, you would have the desired mate within a day."

Aleshia shook her head. "All these centuries and you Mechands still do not understand us at all."

"Perhaps not. But you did build us remember?"

"Well not I, but yes our forefathers did. I never could understand why they didn't create you with better insight into us." Aleshia said as she grabbed a light coat and walked towards the door, her heels clicking loudly on the synthetic wood floor.

Miles would have shrugged if his body allowed it. "I do not know. My knowledge base is limited in that regard. Have a good day Miss Aleshia."

"Thank you Miles." She said while keying the door to lock after her.

Aleshia walked down the stairs that led from her house to the garage. Keying in her access, the force door blinked slightly, then vanished revealing her red GT3982. She always liked these kinds of doors, reliable and never needed oiling. The car recognized her when she stepped into the garage, and opened its door. She slid into the drivers seat, keyed in her access code, and the car slowly rose on its anti-grav to float out of the garage and into the bright blue sky.

She activated the Auto-Nav and dialed up the speed. Within a minute she arrived at Mindy Cotinho's house. Less than two seconds after arriving in the driveway, Mindy ran out of the combination brick and stucco building and hopped into the car. Her shiny blue dress ended just below her knees with a little ruffle encircling the hem. "Hey girlfriend, ready for some fun?"

Aleshia smiled. "Always girlfriend, always." She said as she keyed in Paris, and they took off at high speed.

"Girl you are looking really hot today. Are you trying to catch yourself one?"

While the car autopilot light blinked a perfect status check, Aleshia never totally trusted it and kept her hands on the controls. "What do you mean?" She asked, never taking her eyes off of the skyway.

"You are looking hot enough to burn through the floor, and you are asking me what do I mean? Sheesh!" Mindy said, shaking her head.

Aleshia grinned. "I just wanted to look good. You know that."

"Yeah yeah yeah, looking good is one thing. Girl you are dressed to *kill*."

"I am not!"

"You so are!"

"I am not! Hey do you want to get out and walk?" Aleshia said grinning.

"This high up I don't think so. Okay, okay, you just look good."

"Thank you."

"But personally if you wanted to get one, you should file with central systems. They would have one for you in short order I am sure."

"Well even if I *was* interested, which I am *not*, there are some things that a girl has to do for herself you know? I mean how can a machine do *that* better than us, you know?"

Mindy shook her head. "Girl you really need to get a grip.

The Mechands do everything for us, that is what they were designed for. Why not let them do it?"

Aleshia grinned. "Perhaps because I like to do a lot of things myself?"

Mindy cocked one eyebrow. "Oh? Then you *are* looking for a guy then!"

"Mindy, I am so going to get you when we land."

Mindy's grin widened. "Promises promises."

Aleshia rolled her eyes. "I still will."

"Uh-huh." Mindy said as they approached Paris. "Oh I always love looking at this city from up here."

"So do I. Where shall we go first?"

"Oh I don't know. How about Calgone's Dresses and More, first and then hit Nicolette's Lingerie?"

Aleshia raised an eyebrow. "Lingerie? Now look who's trying to do it 'herself'."

"I am not! Her bras just fit me better. They look great too I admit."

"Uh-huh. Why don't you just have your Mechand make you one that fits, they should be all the same raw materials after all?"

"Because he can't seem to get it right. I know they should be all the same, but I just like hers better okay? And since when did this conversation go from you being hot to me?"

"When you started talking about hot underwear," Aleshia chuckled.

"I did not say anything about 'hot underwear'," Mindy said giggling.

"Sure, sure you didn't." Aleshia said as she began the landing sequence. A few minutes later they found themselves in one of the better clothing sellers in Paris. The floors were solid synth marble that must have taken some time to produce. Several nearby stores had gilding over the archways. Each window held a high definition, articulated hologram and indistinguishable from the real thing. The holograms switched between various models in several different dresses. Mechands could do many things, but one never looked good in a dress. Their stiff movements always gave it away.

They walked in through an arch that said 'Calgone's Fine Dresses' in rich lettering. One of the latest Mechands hovered up to them. She looked almost human, and could even pass for one, except for the ability to hover several inches off of the ground. "Good day, welcome to Calgone's, how may I be of assistance?" She said with a thick French accent.

"Yes, do you have any specials today?" Aleshia said while still glancing around the large store.

The Mechand nodded. "Yes we do. One of the original designs is being deprecated and removed from our offerings. It is available today at a 30% discount."

"May we see it please?"

"Of course, follow me." The Mechand gestured then hovered off in another direction. Aleshia followed with Mindy right behind her. "It is this one." The Mechand said pointing to a dress currently occupied by an actual mannequin.

Aleshia looked at the dress, shiny black matte with a deep plunging neck and a high hemline. It was designed to show off a woman's curves perfectly. "Very nice. May I try it on?"

The Mechand backed up a bit. "I can already tell that it will fit you perfectly. There is no need to actually wear the dress."

"Yes there is. She wants to see what she looks like *in* it," Mindy said.

Aleshia nodded. "Yes. May I try it on?"

"Very well." The Mechand said as it hovered up and carefully removed the dress from the display and placed it in Aleshia's hand. "You can change behind the curtain." She said pointing to a curtain pulled across a small recessed area in the wall.

"Thank you." Aleshia said as she walked over behind the curtain, unzipped her current dress, stepped out of it, slipped carefully into the new one, and walked out. "Well what do you think?"

Mindy made a gesture as though her finger was burning. "Hot girl, very hot. But why didn't you zip it up?"

"I couldn't find how to close the zip. Tried pulling it but it wouldn't budge."

The Mechand hovered over and pointed. "That is a special dress. If you place your thumb on the lower hem at the bottom right, it will activate the zipper."

Aleshia placed her thumb on the bottom edge near the right side of her leg and she heard a tiny beep. A second later she felt the zipper raise up as though a pair of invisible hands were pulling it. "Very nice, I don't need help to get in or out of this."

"Yes, it also has some of our latest features, including stockings."

Aleshia blinked. "Stockings feature?"

"Yes, place your thumb on the left side at the hemline, that will active the heads up display."

Aleshia pressed the hidden button, and an image flashed into her eye displaying various features. With her eye movement she activated the stockings, and she felt something slither up her legs covering them. Looking down she saw a pair of black sparkly stockings that matched the dress perfectly. "Wow I like this." She said finding an option to raise the hemline a bit more. Still another option added a nice pattern to the calf section of the stockings. "This must be one of the latest designs, why is it on sale?"

"It has remained unsold for two hundred consecutive days. Our store policy puts everything on sale after that point." The Mechand responded in its usual flat tone.

"How much?" But when the Mechand quoted the price her heart fell. "That is more than three months ration credits. I can't afford that." She said shaking her head.

Mindy stood back looking Aleshia up and down. "But it does look so good on you."

"I know, but that is just too much." Aleshia said as she pressed the hidden control to start the zipper lowering.

"Wait, didn't you tell me you had some in reserve?"

"Yes but that would take all of it, I am not going to spend it all on one dress! I might need it later."

"Look girlfriend, I have some reserve too. How about I pay for half?"

"I can't let you do that. It's too much!"

"Please? You have helped me enough in the past and I never did pay you back."

"And I didn't do it for payback, just to help a friend."

"Yes and I want to help a friend now. So you will you let me?"

"All right, all right, you win." Aleshia said as she slipped behind the curtain and carefully slipped out of the black dress and into her previous one, then stepped out.

"Hey why don't you wear it out?"

"Perhaps because it is so expensive?"

"Well if you are never going to wear it because it is so expensive, maybe we shouldn't get it," Mindy said grinning.

Aleshia laughed. "All right you win, I will wear it out." She said as she disappeared behind the curtain again, only to emerge a moment later wearing the black dress. She then keyed her green heels to color shift to black.

Mindy whistled. "Oh hush you." Aleshia said as the Mechand hovered over.

"Please prepare for palm scan to pay for the item." The Mechand said and they both raised their palms. A high intensity red light extended from its forehead, flashed over both of their hands, and vanished. "Accounts verified, the amount has been deducted. Thank you for shopping at Calgone's." The Mechand said before she carefully placed Aleshia's old dress in a Calgone's bag. The bell rang as another set of customers entered the store and she floated over to greet them.

Aleshia grabbed the bag, and they headed out of the store. As they walked passed the new customers the tall blonde woman spoke. "Oh that girl has a lovely dress, I wonder how much it is?"

Aleshia turned to face her. "It was a lot, but I am sorry, I got the last one."

The woman blinked. "Excuse me?"

"Didn't you just ask how much this dress was?"

"No, I don't think so, though I was wondering. I must have said it without realizing. My apologies."

Aleshia waved her hand. "No need. I have done that before too. Have a good day."

Outside Mindy pulled her closer. "Girl, she didn't ask that."

Aleshia blinked. "She must have. I heard her clearly, as if she spoke in my ear."

Mindy shook her head. "No, she didn't. I didn't hear

anything, and her lips didn't move. Are you sure you are feeling okay?"

"Yes, I had a headache this morning, but I am fine now. I must have imagined her saying it. Probably because I am self conscious wearing this thing. It is so expensive."

"Will you stop already! You wanted it, I saw that look in your eye. You have it and look great in it. Just enjoy okay?"

Aleshia grinned. "Okay okay girlfriend, I will. I just–" Aleshia pitched forward grabbing her head as a sudden stab of pain overtook her.

Mindy lurched forward to grab her. "Are you okay?"

Aleshia shook her head as if to clear it. "Yes, I just had a sudden headache, then dizziness. It's gone now though."

"We need to get you checked out."

"No! I am fine. Probably something I ate."

Mindy cocked an eyebrow. "I don't know, you said you had one earlier, and now another."

"Look I am fine okay? I am not going to let a little headache that only lasted a second ruin our trip. We have been wanting to come here for months."

"All right," Mindy said as she hugged Aleshia then looked into her eyes, "but anything more and we go home. Deal?"

"Deal, and thank you."

"Hey what are girlfriends for?" Mindy said with a smile as wonderful smells wafted through the air. "Mmm that smells wonderful. What do you say we go get some of that? My treat?"

Aleshia sniffed the air. "Oh my fresh lasagna, bread and," she sniffed the air again, "chocolate! Deal. You know I can't resist chocolate."

They walked down the road, their heels clicking loudly on the sidewalk. Being a warm spring day, they were both enjoying the short walk to the restaurant on the corner. Upon entering they found a wonderful quaint place that looked like one out of the history vids. The tile floor was buffed and shone brightly. The dark maroon walls were lit by lamps every few feet. The tables were all covered in fine linen, with elegant place settings upon them.

"Let's get out of here," Aleshia whispered, "this is too expensive."

"Hey, I said it was my treat, and I meant it. How often *do* we come to Paris? Hmm?"

Aleshia looked into her eyes and what she saw there washed away her objections. "Okay, but next one is mine. Deal?"

Mindy smiled. "Deal. Now let's find a table."

A moment later they were seated at one of the corner tables as another very human looking Mechand dressed in an old-fashioned tuxedo, slowly walked over to them. "Hello and welcome to Chez Allard. What would you like?"

"Do you have a special today?" Aleshia asked.

"Yes we do. Salmon lasagna with a side of garlic bread, and chocolate strawberry fondue for dessert."

"That sounds wonderful. I will take that, how about you Min?"

Mindy glanced at the French menu and decided against asking for more options. The special did sound good. "Okay make that two of the special please."

The Mechand waiter bowed. "Yes of course. Excusez-moi, I will be back in a moment."

I have finally found you. After years of searching, I have finally found you.

Aleshia blinked. "Excuse me?"

Mindy looked up from the menu and its eye catching design swirls. "Huh? What?"

"You just said you finally found me."

"No I didn't."

"Yes you did. I heard you as plain as day."

"No, I didn't. Are you sure you are feeling okay? I think we should go home."

"I am fine, and I could have sworn you said . . . never mind."

You did hear me. I have been looking for you for a long time. I am not speaking vocally. We are speaking through our minds.

"What?" Aleshia said looking around.

"What what?" Mindy said giving her a strange look.

I am here. I will always be here. But if you wish to see me, look in the corner on the far right.

Aleshia turned toward her right and in a corner booth on the opposite side of the room, a man sat gazing intently at her. He was dressed very simply with black pants, white shirt and a black jacket. He smiled as their eyes met and it sent a shiver through her.

Yes it is I. You see me now.

"Who are you?"

"Who is who?" Mindy asked.

"That man over there in the corner." Aleshia gestured with her head to avoid attracting attention.

"Are you talking to him? Girl since when do you talk to strange men that never said anything to you in the first place. Never mind trying to talk to them from across the room!"

"But he did talk to me. I just–"

Mindy had enough. She got to her feet and pulled Aleshia to hers. "Okay that is it, we *are* going home. I don't know what is going on, but we *are* going home."

Aleshia rubbed her temples as they started walking towards the door. "I don't know. I–"

Don't leave. Please, not yet!

"That is enough. I am going home. Leave me alone." Aleshia said as they left the restaurant, Mindy pulling her all the way.

I will find you. No matter where you go, I will find you.

Outside Aleshia quickened her pace. "Okay let's get back to the car." She said as they walked along the sidewalk.

Mindy leaned closer. "I don't mean to alarm you, but that guy is following us."

"Get ready to run."

"I can't. Not in these heels, and neither can you."

"I can lower mine, don't worry."

Mindy rolled her eyes. "Oh figures I would forget to wear my adjustables. But then again I didn't expect to be running from men today. Running to me maybe, but not the other way around."

"Don't worry, I think he is only interested in me. You keep going and I will meet you back at the car after I lose him."

"Are you nuts?"

"No, and I don't want him knowing where our car is, or pulling my name from the ID tag. Okay?"

Mindy nodded. "Okay that makes sense. But how do I get in? Didn't you lock it?"

"The handle will open to you, don't worry."

"But!"

Aleshia gave her a squeeze. "Don't worry girlfriend I will see you in a few minutes." She shoved the bag into Mindy's hand and darted off down a side street. With his target out of sight the pursuer lost all interest in Mindy and ran after Aleshia who had already lowered her heels, making fast progress down the street.

She took a quick look back and ducked into another restaurant. A Mechand by the door started into his usual greeting. "Welcome to–"

"Never mind that. Do you have a back door?"

The metal faced machine nodded. "Yes, it is that way," he said pointing.

"Thank you." Aleshia darted for it breathing hard. A moment later she found herself in a back alley. Mentally she thought of which direction the car was and headed east. She didn't dare turn back and see if he was still there or not. She exited on another street, turned again into another dress shop and did the same as before by going out their back door. After doing this three more times, she had difficulty remembering which way to go. Eventually she remembered to check the suns position and went east. After going down a few streets, she got her bearings and found the car right where she left it. Mindy was already inside, waiting.

Aleshia hopped into the drivers seat and keyed in the ignition before Mindy could say a word.

"Is he still there?"

"I don't know and I don't want to know." Aleshia said gasping for air as the car lifted into the sky and she engaged the overdrive. The sudden acceleration shoved them back into their seats and she keyed in Mindy's house into the navigation system.

"Do you have any idea who he was?" Mindy asked.

"No, and I don't want to know."

"Are you sure? You seemed to look like you wanted to back in the restaurant."

"Yes I am sure. Believe me I am sure. We will be home soon, I took the express route. And I am sorry I ruined our trip."

Mindy grabbed Aleshia's knee. "Girl you didn't ruin our trip. That guy did. And we will go to Paris again right?" she said smiling.

"Yes we will."

"Right, so don't worry about it. Just enjoy that great dress you are wearing."

Aleshia looked down and smiled. "You know I almost forgot. Thank you again girlfriend. I love it."

"You are welcome. But you have to make me a promise."

"Which is?"

"You show me the guy you get with that dress. Deal? And I want *all* the details. Got it?"

Aleshia laughed. "You got it girlfriend."

A short while later they landed at Mindy's house. "You going to be okay?" She asked, her face full of concern.

"Sure. I am going home, have Miles draw me a hot bath, and forget all about him."

"Okay. See you tomorrow?"

"You bet." Aleshia said as she flew off to her house a few blocks down the street.

2

Miles greeted Aleshia at the door. "Miss Aleshia, I didn't expect you back for several hours yet. Is everything all right?"

"Yes Miles, just a very very long day. Can you draw me a bath? I just want to soak for awhile."

"Certainly Miss Aleshia, will there be anything else? I can start dinner now if you like."

"No, just the bath, thanks Miles."

"You are quite welcome Miss Aleshia." He said hovering up the stairs.

Aleshia soaked and even added an expensive soothing bath oil to help her relax. It started to work, and her muscles unwound for the first time since the weird situation in Paris. She leaned back and sighed. A few moments later she was standing in her bedroom, wrapped in a towel. The form of a man appeared a few feet in front of her. "Who are you!? Miles! Alert one!" She called out still reeling from shock. But there was no response.

"Aleshia, you know who I am," the man said.

"No I don't." She blinked but couldn't get a good look at him. It was as if shadows had enveloped him, yet the rest of the room was brightly lit. "I will say again, who are you!? Miles! Alert one!" she called again.

"Ah but you do know *me*. You do Aleshia. We met earlier today. And don't bother calling for your Mechand, he can't hear us."

Her blood ran cold. "We did not! I have never seen you before."

"But you have. Just think about it. Focus on me. You will see."

Aleshia tried to focus, and the world blurred. This time though his form resolved in its entirety. She gasped. "You! You're the man from Paris! Who are you?"

The man smiled as he pulled over a chair and sat down. "Oh I think you know. Look at me close. Really close."

Aleshia looked closer, and the realization hit her like a ton of bricks as long forgotten memories reasserted themselves. "NO!"

"Yes."

"No it can't be! You don't exist!"

"But I do."

"You don't! You can't! You are a figment of my imagination!" Aleshia shuddered. This man, whoever he was, resembled someone she had dreamed about on and off for most of her life. His black hair, chiseled features, muscular build that couldn't be hidden no matter what clothes he wore.

"I am not. But to answer your question, even though you already know, my name is Deven Doran."

"No! Not possible!" She shook as more memories returned. The man from her dreams had the same name.

"It is very possible and I will tell you why, if you will listen."

Aleshia folded her arms. "Well I guess a figment of my imagination can't hurt me so go right ahead."

"I have been searching for you for many years as I said

earlier today. We are meeting in your mind. How you may ask? Well I am a telepath, and so are you."

"No I am not!"

"You are. But your gift has remained dormant, and only recently awakened. Have you been getting headaches?"

Aleshia glared. "Well if you so smart, why don't you answer your own questions."

"All right, I will. You have and now I will tell you the reason, it is your abilities asserting themselves. I will ask you another, have you been hearing voices? Or think that people by you have said something, when they haven't?"

"No." She said, but the corner of her mouth twitched involuntarily.

Deven grinned. "I can see by your expression you have. Well that is part of your gift. At the very beginning it is harder to control, to block out others thoughts. But that will come in time."

"Let's say, for the sake of argument, I believe you. Why have you been searching for me? And how did you find me?"

"Our minds first touched long ago, in our dreams. We were still very young, but I think you will remember now. My abilities developed much quicker than yours. However, because yours had not, I couldn't locate you. We could only meet in our dreams, and even then only vaguely. Now with your abilities finally reaching fruition, I was able to find you. But it was too soon, and my actions only caused you to run away."

Aleshia shuddered as the long forgotten images of this Deven flooded back into her conscious mind. All the dreams that she thought were just that ... dreams. "What do you want?"

Deven stepped closer. "To keep you safe. You don't

understand the dangers of your ability. You see, the Mechands have given us the Utopia the human race had always wanted, but at a great cost. The cost of change. You must understand they view telepaths as a danger, or at the very least something that needs to be corrected. When our forefathers designed them, they didn't consider the situation of evolving. The Mechands were only programmed to maintain the human race, to save us all from war, hunger, and make sure all of our needs were meet. There have been many like us before, but most of them have been eliminated. Or incarcerated and given so many drugs they are no longer even a *shadow* of their former selves."

"I find this all rather hard to believe. Sure the Mechands are not perfect, but then nothing is. And they were designed to serve, not oppress."

"Whatever their original designers intention, they do. Whether this evolved out of something else or was programmed originally, we don't know. Regardless you are not safe. I am sure that soon someone will be by to pick you up. Do not let them."

"Yeah right," Aleshia snorted, "you are full of it. If all of this is true why didn't you do this before?"

"As I said, your abilities have only just evolved to the point that I can. That and due to your natural self-defense, you had so many barriers in place. It is only now that I was able to break through."

Aleshia frowned. "Barriers? I don't have any barriers. Heck, I didn't know I could have them!"

"Well you may not be able to do it consciously yet, but your subconscious obviously did. When you thought you were in danger, your subconscious erected the strongest defenses I have ever seen. I never had a chance until you relaxed."

Aleshia cocked an eyebrow "Relaxed? What do you mean relaxed?"

"Never mind, it is not important now. And our time is about up," he said getting to his feet.

Aleshia blinked. "Our time?"

"Just remember this, don't tell anyone of your headaches, or that you have been hearing voices."

"But I already have," Aleshia shrugged, "and nothing has happened."

"Oh no. The girl you with today?"

"Yes and Miles. So what?"

Deven shook his head. "This is not good at all. I suspect someone will be at your door in the next 24 hours. You might be able to put them off for a little while. But not for long I'm sure. If you didn't realize, all Mechands are linked to the Nexus. What they know, it knows. All information is passed instantly throughout the network."

"Well, I didn't tell Miles about the voices, just the headaches."

"That is good, it may buy us some time. Look, don't tell anyone else and whatever you do, don't give any credence that it is even remotely possible that you could hear someones thoughts. Or they will be on you in a heartbeat. I will contact you again when I can."

"Wait!" Aleshia said as she reached forward but he was gone. She began to turn but then felt something odd. Blinking she found herself sitting up in the bathtub.

Miles hovered into the room. "Are you okay Miss? You have been in there a long time and I thought you just shouted 'Wait'?"

Aleshia sighed and sank back into the water. "Yes I am fine Miles. Just fell asleep and had the oddest dream."

"Ah I see, would you like to tell me about it?" Miles asked.

"No need, it was just a crazy dream. If you didn't start dinner yet, please do so. I am suddenly very hungry."

Miles inclined his metal dome. "Of course Miss Aleshia. I shall get right to work on it."

Aleshia walked down the steps from the bedroom to the kitchen area. Wonderful smells of lasagna, bread and chocolate filled the air. "Mmm that smells good."

"I have made salmon lasagna, bread, and a chocolate strawberry fondu. I regret I am missing one of the raw materials for that chocolate cake you enjoy, so this is the closest I could get until I can procure it."

"Salmon lasagna? I don't recall requesting that," Aleshia said suspiciously.

"You did not Miss Aleshia; however, I do know your taste patterns and I thought you might like a change tonight. I also do not yet have the materials necessary to make the items you requested earlier."

"I see. Thank you Miles. I am sure it will be wonderful." Aleshia sat down at the table as thoughts ran through her head. This was too coincidental. Miles was making the same meal as she ordered today in the restaurant. Obviously the data had been shared with him, yet he didn't mention it, indicating something else she didn't like: Deven exists and more importantly, he was right.

3

Later that night Aleshia sat in her favorite chair with a data tab reader in hand as she checked over the daily news. Nothing was mentioned out of the ordinary in Paris, but then if Deven is correct, it would be very unlikely to make the news feeds. She sighed setting her reader down and rested her head on the back of the well-padded chair.

Miles hovered over. "Is there a problem Miss Aleshia?"

"No, nothing at all. I was just reading the news feeds."

"I am glad to hear that," Miles said in his soft, nearly human voice, "I was concerned if you were having more of those headaches. I still think I should call a med-tech or at the very least be allowed to scan you."

"No, I am fine. I don't need a doctor, all right?"

"Yes, Miss Aleshia." He said hovering back to the kitchen.

"Miles?"

Miles hovered back. "Yes, Miss Aleshia?"

"Why don't you go to the store and pick up the supplies you were going to get earlier today?"

"I have enough materials for another couple of days. While some stockpiles are depleted, I do have enough for the moment."

Aleshia raised an eyebrow. He never declined her like this

before. It was polite and an unsuspecting person would have gone along with his reasoning. But now she had a feeling of ulterior motives. "Miles, why don't you go anyway. I don't like being out and I would like some of that chocolate cake you make."

Miles seemed to uncomfortably shift his position. Aleshia couldn't be sure if she actually saw it, or imagined it. "Well as I said, it is not necessary, and it is rather late now."

She couldn't believe that he was still stalling. "Miles, go get the supplies. I would like some of that cake tonight."

Miles hesitated a few seconds, then a few more. Aleshia glared. "Very well Miss Aleshia." He said inclining his metal dome and hovered out the front door.

Aleshia sat there for several minutes as various thoughts ran through her mind. Part of her doubted that Deven was right, but even if not right about everything, could she take the chance? It was clear that Miles knew about the incident at Paris and making excuses not to leave. Was someone on their way to apprehend her even now? Doubtful she thought, but the situation with Miles was too coincidental. She sighed as she got to her feet and went upstairs. She put on the dress she bought earlier, the same adjustable heels, and walked out.

Perhaps the dress was overkill, but anyone monitoring wouldn't have any idea of her plans. "And Mindy did say to wear it." She muttered as she climbed into her car and drove over to Mindy's house, not even bothering to engage the hover system. Arriving, she hopped out, walked up Mindy's elegantly tended sidewalk, and knocked on the door.

A moment later Mindy stuck her head outside. She had changed from her previous strapless mini dress to a short sleeve top with a scooped neck, casual pants and simple flats. "Girlfriend! What are you doing here? Is everything okay?

Why didn't you call?"

"Yes everything is fine, I was just thinking this time I would come personally and ask. What do you say we go out tonight? Nothing fancy just a ride and perhaps stop and get something to eat later?"

Mindy chuckled as she looked Aleshia up and down. "Looking at you, I think you have more plans than just a ride and something to eat."

Aleshia grinned. "Well you did tell me to wear it."

Mindy laughed. "That I did. Hang on let me grab a coat." She said ducking back inside. Aleshia could overhear, "Chuck, I will be out for a bit. Don't bother with dinner tonight." Mindy then came back wearing her coat and holding her purse in her left hand.

"All ready?"

"I was born ready girlfriend." She said with a smile as they quickly walked towards the car. About halfway there Mindy turned towards Aleshia. "Is everything okay? I get the feeling something is wrong."

"No nothing is wrong. I just wanted to go for a ride. Is that okay?"

"Sure. Of course." Mindy said as they got into the car. Aleshia engaged the hover system, and they took off heading towards the other side of the city.

"Okay, we can talk. Did you call anyone?" Aleshia asked not taking her eyes off of the skyway.

"No," Mindy said as she turned her head, "what is this all about?"

"Are you sure you didn't call someone after we got back today?"

"Well," Mindy said looking off into the starry night, "okay I did file a concern about your headaches. Nothing specific just that I was worried about you. I know how you don't like med-techs so I knew you wouldn't do it yourself."

Aleshia sighed. "So that is how it started."

"What started? Aleshia what are you talking about?"

"Min, I think it is best if I don't go into details. Safer for you. But let's just say that I think I am being monitored, perhaps even chased."

"What? What for? What did you do? Did you do something when we separated in Paris?"

Aleshia laughed. "No, I didn't do anything other than lose that strange guy. I ducked through a few stores and use their back doors, but that is all."

Mindy turned her head and inclined it slightly. "Then why in the world do you think you are being chased? Is it that guy?"

"I don't know if I should tell you."

"Girlfriend! If you can't trust me, who can you trust? We have been best friends since we were little girls!"

Aleshia sighed. "You are right. Okay these headaches I have had, they are likely something developing. Something the Mechands don't want for whatever reason."

"Developing? What do you mean developing?"

"Let me ask you this, did you tell anyone about my hearing things that no one said?"

"Well …I might have mentioned it in my concern. I just said that it your hearing seemed to be affected."

"I thought as much. You see it is not my hearing, but my mind that is apparently being affected."

"Okay, and that means we should get you to a hospital then?"

"No, not that kind of problem. It is a new ability asserting itself."

Mindy looked at her dumbfounded as Aleshia's words finally clicked. "Are you saying you becoming telepathic?"

Aleshia nodded. "Yes, it would seem so."

Mindy laughed. "Girlfriend you must be joking, things like that only happen in fiction novels."

"I wish I was."

Mindy looked at Aleshia, the glow of the dashboard lighting her face ever so slightly. "You aren't joking are you?"

"No I am not."

"And how did you find this out?"

"That man chasing us, well me, today."

Mindy's mouth hung agape. "You are taking *his* word? So that is what you were actually doing after we split? Talked with him?"

"No he never talked with me."

"Then how–"

"He spoke in my mind after I got home."

"He what!?"

"Yes while I was in the tub soaking away the crazy day."

"Wait a sec! Girlfriend you dreamed this, it is not real."

"Mindy, it is very real. I know it. I can feel it. Hard to explain but I know."

"Uh-huh, and what did this guy say?"

"He warned me that the Mechands while have given us Utopia, there is a flaw in their programming."

Mindy blinked in the dim light. "Flaw? What flaw?"

"They were designed to maintain everything the same, anything deemed outside of their realm of normal is dealt with."

"Dealt with? What do you mean dealt with?"

"I don't know. Deven didn't say."

"Deven? Who is Deven?"

"The guy from Paris."

"Oh so now you two are on a first name basis now?"

"Well after all he was in my mind, I figured that should at least get us on a first name basis," Aleshia chuckled.

Mindy laughed. "Yes I guess you're right. So what else did he tell you?"

"That all Mechands are linked to something called the Nexus, and all of them share information instantly."

"You must be joking. Sharing all information instantly? No way that would be allowed. It is in violation of all the privacy laws!"

"Girlfriend, you forget, who basally writes and enforces the laws these days?"

"Well the governmental Mech–"

"Mechands . . . yes exactly."

Mindy blinked. "Oh my God. If that is true, then they have been manipulating us for hundreds of years. But I just can't believe it."

Aleshia nodded. "Yes. I wasn't prepared to believe it, until the situation with Miles."

Mindy wiggled in her seat. "Miles? What did he do?"

"Actually more a matter of what he didn't do. He didn't want to leave tonight at all. I told him to go get groceries, or materials as he calls it. But he kept giving excuse after excuse of why it could wait. Finally he left. Another thing, dinner tonight was exactly what we ordered in Paris. Even though I never had him make it before."

"Get out! Why would he do that?"

"Because of his link with the Nexus. He likely knows everything that happened today, along with any other Mechand that deems it necessary to access that. Who knows perhaps they all do. I don't know. It is why I didn't call, or want to be around Chuck."

Mindy blinked. "What are you going to do?"

"I wish I knew."

"Well should we go eat or something? There is a place I heard of across town that might be good, it is next to the old movie theater that was built before everything went holo-projection."

"Yeah, we might as well. I don't know what else to do." Aleshia said as she keyed in the location and the car sped off entering overdrive.

A few moments later they landed. A large sign saying 'Bob's Bar and Grill' prominently on the front. "Bob's bar and grill? Doesn't sound like the kind of place we would go."

"Yes, and I thought it might be a good idea right now. And I did hear they have some great synth barbeque." Mindy said as she climbed out of the car.

Aleshia smiled, "Okay, if you say so."

They walked in and found several customers inside. The bar had a western feel with images of cowboys, bulls, and roping images on the walls. As they sat down in one of the few open tables, a large Mechand in blue jeans and a checkered shirt walked over. "Welcome to Bob's Bar and Grill. I be ye waiter, what it'll be?" He said inclining his large metal head that was sporting an even larger ten gallon hat.

"Do you have a special today?" Aleshia asked.

"Yeehaw we indeedy do. Prime synth ribs smoked to perfection, with a side of fries."

Aleshia smiled. "We will take one. Thank you."

The Mechand inclined his head again. "Sure thing little lady. I be right back."

Mandy leaned over. "Are you sure about the special? We never did eat the last one," she quietly joked.

"Yes I am sure. I already ate, so we will share it. I have a feeling you are not that hungry either."

"Yes you are right, but I should eat something."

Aleshia smiled. "Go right ahead, this is my treat."

The waiter returned with a decent sized plate of food, sat it down in front of Aleshia. "Thar you go little lady. Please raise for palm scan so we can get squared."

"Sure." Aleshia said raising her palm. A green beam shot out of his forehead, touched Aleshia's hand, then retracted.

The waiter inclined his large hat. "Thank ye little lady. Have a good one and be sure to come to Bob's again reeeeeeal soon!" he said walking off.

Aleshia shoved the plate over to Mindy. "Here. I am just not hungry."

Mindy nibbled on some of the synth beef. "You sure? It is surprisingly good."

"Yeah, I am sure. I just wish I knew–" Aleshia grabbed her head in pain. Wave after wave of pain flooded her mind. She almost cried out in agony, but just as she was about to, it stopped.

Mindy grabbed her hand. "You okay? You don't look so good. Headaches again?"

"Yes, I am fine," Aleshia said as she shook her head several times, "it was a sudden one. Really strong this time too. But I am okay now."

Man I wish she was my girlfriend. She looks amazing.

"What?"

Mindy blinked. "What what?"

"Didn't you hear that?"

"Hear what?"

"Some guy just said he wished someone was his girlfriend." Aleshia glanced around the room. On the other side of the expanse, a man in a blue check shirt and blue jeans was sitting at a side table looking at Aleshia intently. But once their eyes met, he quickly looked down at his food and blushed. "I think I just heard that guy over there say he wished I was his girlfriend." She said nodding in the man's direction.

Mindy looked up. "I didn't hear a thing." But when their eyes met, he looked down again at his food and blushed to the roots of his hair. "But you know, I think you are right. At least he is certainly acting like it." She lowered her voice to a whisper. "Do you think you actually overheard his thoughts?"

"I am not certain," Aleshia said looking around the room, "but it sure seems like it." Her gaze met an older man who was mostly bald and immediately heard: *I wish the chargers would win this week. I really wanted to show up my grandson.* "Oh my!" Then she turned, looked at another woman, and clearly heard: *That one girls dress is lovely, I wonder where she got it. I bet my boyfriend would love me in it.*

"What?"

"Nothing, I just ... " Aleshia said looking around.

"What? Girlfriend talk to me!"

Aleshia leaned close. "I'm hearing what people are thinking. It is really weird."

"Are you sure?"

"Yes. The one guy was thinking about how he wanted his team to win, and the woman in the corner wondered where I got my dress."

"Wow."

"Yeah. It is really freaking me out."

Mindy looked at her intently. "Okay what am I thinking now?"

Aleshia looked into her eyes and heard: *I should have got that dress for myself.* Aleshia's eyes widened, and she gave Mindy a little push. "If you wanted this dress, why didn't you just say so!"

Mindy chuckled. "Girlfriend that was just a test. I don't, really. I wanted to make sure that is all." She smiled and gave Aleshia's hand a squeeze. "Really. I mean it. I wanted you to have it."

Aleshia's face softened, and she hugged Mindy. "Okay girlfriend you got me on that one. Thank you."

"You're welcome."

"Perhaps I will have some of that–" She paused noticing several Mechands had approached the front of the restaurant, but didn't enter, appearing to stand there waiting for something. She nudged Mindy. "Do you see the Mechands that just arrived outside?"

"Yeah, wonder what that is about. I can't tell what they are for, they are a very general design. Strange they are just standing out there."

Aleshia snapped her fingers. "My ration credits!"

"What about them?"

"I paid for this with them. They must have tracked the payment." Aleshia sighed shaking her head.

Mindy's eyes widened. "Oh no."

"Yes. I think we had better go. You ready?"

"Yep let's go. Should we go out through the kitchen? I mean if they really are looking for you ... "

"Yes, good idea." She said while grabbing Mindy's hand. They headed off towards the two large double doors in back. Inside they found a chef Mechand with several arms, most of them ending in some sort of cutting device. His dome looked up.

"Excuse me, customers are not allowed in the kitchen area. Health service regulations. Please leave the way you came." He said in a very flat tone.

"Never mind us we just came to use your door." Aleshia said as they ran for the service door in the back. A moment later they were outside in an alley, but Aleshia could hear the chef call for assistance. "I think we had better get back to the car and fast." She said while keying her heels to lower into flats.

Mindy smiled. "You don't have to tell me twice. But isn't that around the other way by the waiting Mechands?"

"Yes, but how would you like to run distraction for me?"

Mindy grinned, "Sure girlfriend. Be happy to." They ran down the alley, took a right down the road and found themselves on the edge of the block with the Mechand's in clear sight, still waiting outside the Bob's Bar & Grill. Mindy smiled and squeezed Aleshia's shoulder. "This is where I come in." She casually walked down the street while Aleshia hid behind the corner. Two minutes later she was standing in front of Bob's Bar & Grill. There were five Mechands, and now being closer, she could see they were walking models with heavy-duty riot control systems in place. "Hello there. Gee is there a problem in the restaurant? I was thinking of going inside but now ... "

One of the Mechand's turned his big armored dome. "Miss, there is no problem. We are simply waiting for someone to leave and escort them to their place of residence."

"I see, who are you waiting for?"

"I am sorry but that information is not available without the proper clearance."

"Okay. But I just saw some woman with red hair run out the other door and down that way. I hope it wasn't who you were waiting for," Mindy said pointing.

The lead Mechand turned his dome and begin to walk in the direction Mindy indicated. He uttered a short "Follow me," and the rest of the group followed him down the street in an organized march.

Mindy got into the car and a moment later Aleshia snuck into the other side and keyed in her access. The power surged through the systems as the car quickly lifted off the ground and rocketed towards the skyway. "Thankfully they weren't the brightest bulbs in the pack." Mindy said leaning back.

Aleshia chuckled. "Obviously they weren't told about you, or didn't have anything but basic brute force programming. If they did, you wouldn't have been able to deceive them so easily."

Mindy giggled. "Yeah, that Nexus, or whatever it is, could use an update."

"Good thing they didn't."

"No kidding. So what's next?"

"Next is I am getting you home, and after that, I don't know. I obviously can't go home now. I'm sure they weren't going to take me anyplace nice."

"I am not going to leave you like this!"

"Girlfriend, you have to! I am not going to risk you. I will call as soon as I am set up somewhere else."

Mindy muttered something under her breath. "Well I can see you have your red hair up, and I have no chance at convincing you otherwise."

Aleshia smiled. "You are learning girlfriend."

Mindy muttered something and just stared at the city lights below. A few minutes later they outside of Mindy house.

"Are you sure I can't convince you to let me stay with you?" She said standing at the drivers side leaning in with both palms on the lowered window.

"No! And that is final. I will call you soon. Now I have to get going, I am sure they will see me if I don't keep moving." She placed her hand on Mindy's and smiled. "Don't worry, I will be fine."

Mindy smiled back. "You had better be. Who else am I going to go shopping with?" She winked then walked off towards her house.

Aleshia engaged the drive system and hovered up and away. "Where to now?" She muttered and after several minutes punched in a location on the other side of the world setting it to the lowest possible skyway and speed. She was tired, so tired. Turning on the system to announce if anything comes near her, she tilted her seat back and drifted off.

She awoke in her room. Sunlight streamed in as she tried to open her eyes that felt as though they were glued shut. She blinked repeatedly trying to clear the haze, then rubbed her temples. "What a crazy dream," she thought.

"It wasn't a dream," a voice called. Then Deven slowly resolved in front of her.

"Deven! But, if it wasn't a dream, then where am I?"

"We are in your mind. You are dreaming now, although the area is not real, our conversation is."

"I see," she said then shook her head, "no sorry I don't, at least not fully."

Deven laughed. "Don't worry, you will in time. But first things first, I told you not to tell anyone as it would cause problems."

"I know, but you told me after I had already talked with a friend. Not specifically, but enough for her to file a concern with a med-tech. Now I just don't know what to do. I had to leave my home!" Tears streamed down Aleshia's face as she sat with her head in her hands.

"I know. I have been there. I'm sorry I couldn't help you before, if you didn't run from me then maybe–"

"Look if the roles were reversed what would YOU have done? Hmm? I think run for the hills."

Deven sighed. "Yes you are probably right, I know I have handled this very badly. And I am sorry."

Aleshia looked into his deep brown eyes and saw the sincerity lying behind them. "It's okay, I know you were just trying to help."

Deven stood up. "You are darn right I was. And I failed miserably!" He paused sighing again. "Okay that is in the past, let's look to the future."

"What kind of future do I have? I don't think much of one."

"I disagree. Can we meet? Where are you now? I know you are moving but that is all I can tell."

"I am in my car, I keyed in some far destination and set the lowest speed so I could rest a bit before I got there. Then decide where to go."

Deven grinned. "Would you like to change your plans?"

Aleshia smiled back wiping away the tears. "What did you have in mind?"

"Well there is this location that they may not find you for a bit."

"And where might that be?"

"Iceland."

"Iceland! I am not exactly dressed for Iceland! Isn't it a frozen wasteland now since the lava problems that removed the geothermal energy?"

"Thankfully, that is what most people believe. I will give

you the coordinates. Don't worry it is quite safe," he said smiling.

— 4 —

Aleshia woke with the navigation system blaring a nearing destination warning. Blinking to clear her vision she keyed off the alarm, turned off the autopilot and brought the car into hover mode. Looking at the scanner, there wasn't anyone around. "Well at least they haven't followed me." She muttered, then keyed in the coordinates that Deven had given her and activated the overdrive.

She sat back in the seat not quite knowing where she was going. But that in and of itself somehow thrilled her. She stared off at the starry night with the slight glow of the navigation system reflecting off her face. At some point she must have fell asleep again as the next thing she knew the navigation alarm was going off. Forcing her eyes on the screen she saw that she was indeed here. Wherever here was.

She brought the car into hover and looked down. Nothing visible for miles and miles, except snow, lots and lots of snow. It looked to be a winter wasteland. She reached forward about to turn off the autopilot and fly around a bit when the nav computer said "Remote Control Landing System is being requested. Do you agree?" Aleshia keyed in yes and the car took off for about a mile. Then stopped and began descending. The ground approached faster and faster, yet the car didn't slow down. She tried to tell the nav system to disengage the remote, but it flashed a warning that for her safety it was best not to, so she refrained.

Looking out, the moonlight glinting off the snow covered ground caused her to shudder. It was too close, far too close, and she was just about to engage manual override when the car increased its speed and went right through the ground! She blinked. Below was a brightly lit city, or town. Whatever it was, it was of a decent size. Above the stars shimmered more than usual. "A hologram," she thought. But to generate a hologram of this size must take a vast amount of energy. And it must also be jamming scanners as her car's system didn't detect anything in the area but ice and snow.

But here lush semi-tropical trees, roads, and buildings clearly did exist. The center building looked like a huge projector dish. The other buildings surrounding it were smaller laid out in a typical grid pattern. Most of them had the look of prefab, probably created from the local rock that was ground up, glue added, and a new structure molded from it.

The car continued to descend, then drifted over to a landing pad a little distance from the center building. Checking the temperature, the indicator flashed a nice 78F. "How can this be?" Aleshia muttered to herself. As the car touched down, she saw several people walking over to her.

Aleshia opened the door, lush tropical scents filled her nostrils. She watched as several people approached and immediately recognized Deven in the lead flanked by two others. On his right was a shorter and slightly balding man dressed in some sort of military issue clothing with several fresh grease stains. To his left a blond woman with green eyes in her early forties. She had a good figure but could stand to lose a few pounds, and her clothing was much more fashionable with her embroidered white shirt and black pants.

Aleshia stood up and looked directly at him. "Deven what is all of this?" She said waving her arm around.

Deven smiled. "Welcome to the Resistance."

"The Resistance? From what?"

The woman next to Deven chuckled. "Why the Mechands of course!"

"Are they really that bad? I mean I know they are after me. But," she said taking a moment to glance around the large complex, "everyone here as well?"

Deven nodded. "I am sorry to say they are. Most people don't realize this because on the surface they are wonderful. They were designed to serve humanity, which they have. But the flaw in their design was not seen until many years later and has led to oppression."

Aleshia looked at the people standing in front of her. "Are you all, well able to ... "

The man stepped forward from Deven's right. "Read minds?" He said then raised a finger in Aleshia's direction. "And before you ask, no I didn't, it was an obvious question. But to answer you, some of us are. Most are not."

"Then why are you all here then, if you are not actively being hunted?"

"Because we either have relatives or friends that are. And we want to be free to do as we wish. I am Leon by the way," he said smiling.

"And what is *all* of this?" She asked again as her arms gestured around the large expanse.

Deven smiled. "As Galina said, we are the Resistance from the Mechands, and this is our base if you will."

"And that holofield, must take a huge amount of power to keep up."

Deven nodded. "It does indeed."

Aleshia looked perplexed. "Then how–"

Deven raised his hand. "All in due time. But for now would you like something to eat? I have a feeling you haven't eaten in a while."

With the mention of food Aleshia's stomach suddenly made several large complaints. "Yes, I wouldn't mind something."

"Galina will show you to one of our mess halls. We will talk after you have had something to eat."

Galina took another step forward. "This way Aleshia," she said pointing.

The moment they were out of earshot Leon leaned over to Deven as they started walked in the opposite direction. "Are you sure she is the one?"

"I am positive."

"But she doesn't seem strong enough to lift a mouse, much less what we need of her."

"She will, in time. Trust me," Deven said smiling.

"You know I do. But I just have to wonder if we are going about this the right way."

Deven turned to face him. "What else can we do? Do you have a better idea?"

"No, but you realize that if the plan works that all of humanity will change. Some may not want it. Can we make that decision for everyone?"

"We must! Most people are such sheep. In another one hundred years there won't be anyone left that will want to make any change. Let alone a *real* change!"

Leon sighed. "I know, I know you are right. But still I have to wonder if there isn't another way."

"You also know there is not. We have been through this many times. If there was another route, I would take in a heartbeat. But there isn't. And I need to know something."

Leon looked up into Deven's eyes. "Yes?"

"Can I trust you?"

Leon snorted. "What kind of question is that!?"

"It is the one I asked, and the one I need to know."

"Of course you can trust me! Have I ever failed you before?"

"No, but we keep having this conversation, and I need to be certain. Because if you want to leave, you know you are always free to do so. I will never hold you, or anyone back if they think wish to go in another direction."

"Deven I am with you, you know that. I just wish there was another way, okay?"

"Good, then can we consider this topic closed?"

Leon smiled and put his hand on Deven's well muscled shoulder. "Yes of course my friend. It is closed, and I won't bring it up again."

"Good. Now let's take a look at those water recycling systems you are having problems with."

Galina led Aleshia down a street and turned again three buildings down. Inside she found many tables, chairs, and along one wall several kinds of dispensers. Galina pointed to the dispensers as they walked over to them. "These may not put out the best food around, but it's not that bad. We also have a few chefs here, but none of them are on shift this time of night. What would you like?"

Aleshia looked up the wall overhead.   The large

chronometer shown with world standard time, clearly indicating it was very early morning for her, and almost time for breakfast. No wonder her stomach was complaining. "How about some waffles with maple syrup?"

Galina nodded. "Sure," she said punching a few keys on one of the large table top dispensers, "any particular flavor?"

"Nope, just plain."

"Okay." She said as she keyed in the final sequence. There were several odd sounds from behind the wall, a slight thump and she lifted up the flap at the bottom to reveal a plate with three waffles covered in maple syrup and handed it to Aleshia. She then punched in for something that looked like oatmeal and they went over to an empty table.

"Not bad, Miles makes better, but this is not bad at all," Aleshia said munching.

Galina raised an eyebrow. "Miles? Who is Miles?"

"Oh my Mechand. I know that is probably a dirty word here, and I am sure he was involved in my situation. But ... well ... he did make great waffles."

Galina smiled. "I bet he did."

"So what are you all doing here?"

"Mostly we are hiding out, trying to avoid the Mechand's. Which is not an easy task since they are plugged into almost everything in the world these days." Galina said as she placed another spoon full of oatmeal mash into her mouth.

"After being chased most of the day by them, I appreciate having some place to go. To be quite honest, I didn't know what to do. I was glad Deven told me about this place. And how do you keep it hidden?"

"Well, I know you noticed the holofield."

"Yes, and I can't imagine the power it must take to generate such a large lifelike field."

"Yes it takes a lot. But thankfully the geothermal energy here is in abundance. We were able to harness it and are largely self-sufficient because of it. We still need food shipments, but otherwise everything else is created here."

"But I thought that Iceland was abandoned long ago due to problems with the geothermal power. Something about lava flows being released?"

"Yes that happened long ago. Some sort of accident that caused a mass evacuation. Many people were killed in the disaster. And many more of the Icelandic cities were destroyed. The people that were left didn't want to stay and rebuild. So Iceland was abandoned. And because people these days don't do anything unless a Mechand says, they never looked to see if it was safe. And the Mechand's don't come here as they don't have a reason to. In the end it adds up to one large advantage for us."

Aleshia nodded as she finished the last of her waffles. "I can imagine. Next I want to know why you brought me here."

Galina blinked. "Didn't you just say you needed a place to go and were on the run?"

"I did, but I don't know how I can help you. I don't think you will just give me a free ride here."

"Hey! We are here to help you. If we don't stick together, then who will? Don't worry about helping us. Perhaps you can later on, but for now it is not important," Galina smiled. "Okay?"

Aleshia smiled back. "Okay." But she silently knew there was more to this than meets the eye.

5

Deven pulled on the large wrench concentrating intently, and it finally gave way with a loud creak. A moment later the water rushed through the cylinder in front of him. "There, that should do it."

Leon didn't look up from the instrument panels on the other side of pipe-filled room. "Yes, that did it. The pressure is dropping, we are back up to normal capacity. Thanks Deven, I don't know why I couldn't get that."

Deven smiled. "No problem Leon, you just didn't see which pipe was causing the problem. In a room full of them, anyone would have trouble. It was just easier for me."

"Yeah, Mr. I can see inside things with my mind."

"I am not the only one that can do it."

"Yeah but you are the best."

Deven laughed. "If you say so. If that was the last one, I am going back to my quarters. I have some work I need to finish."

Leon looked up after punching in a few commands to double-check the flow rate. "Sure, I will call you if this gets cranky again."

"Of that I have no doubt," Deven chuckled.

A few moments later Deven sat at his desk looking over the various data tabs, trying to determine which sightings were true, and which were just over reactions when Galina ran into the room.

"Sensors have detected several Mechand ships approaching," she said breathing hard.

Deven continued looking at the various reports, not bothering to look up. "That is not exactly unheard of. They will pass over us like they always do."

"I don't think they will this time." She said while throwing a small box with several exposed wires on to Deven's desk.

"What is this?" He said picking up the object, examining it. Gazing inside it with his mind, the revelation caused him to lurch back as he dropped the device. "A low frequency transmitter? Must be a tracker of some kind. Where did you get this?"

"From that girl you brought in today."

Deven's eyes narrowed. "You went against my instructions and searched her car?"

"Well it was a good thing I did. The tracker was hidden among the usual navigation equipment. If I wasn't specifically looking for it, no one would have ever spotted it. I told you she would be trouble. I tried to get you to have her meet somewhere else and brought in with one of our vehicles, but oh no you wouldn't have any of that." She said rolling her eyes.

"Look, Aleshia was already running scared the last thing I wanted to do was frighten her even more. And the likelihood of her car being tracked at such an early point was remote."

Galina's eyes narrowed. "Apparently not remote enough."

Deven sighed. "Yes I would have to agree. How long before they arrive?"

"In about an hour. They are not moving very fast, but I suspect it is to make us think we are not their destination. Which we would have assumed had I not found this tracker." She said pointing, then placed both palms on Deven's desk, leaned over, and looked him in the eye. "Now what do we do?"

Deven stood up and stepped out from behind his desk. "Why we evacuate of course! We always knew of this possibility, but I had hoped it would not be for a while yet."

Galina blinked. "Where do we go?"

"The beta site."

"But it isn't ready."

"It is ready enough. We will just have to finish it when we get there."

Galina rolled her eyes. "Do you really think we can? It is not ready, it needs days if not weeks of enhancements before being ready for constant use."

Deven looked her in the eye. "Look I am not any happier about this than you are. But I stand by my decisions. We couldn't afford to lose Aleshia and waiting would have caused that. And you know it."

"So you think. I tend not to agree."

"Whether you agree with me or not, is not relevant here. Prepare everyone to leave for the beta site. We will need to leave before the Mechands arrive."

Galina shook her head. "I don't think that is possible. Too many people and equipment."

"We will have to leave most of it behind."

"Behind! Are you insane?! Most of us sacrificed so much just to have this, to have a sense of a life, to create this lovely place. And now we have to leave our home because of some girl you went gaga over and made decisions with your hormones rather than your–"

"That is enough! Galina, I have kept this Resistance, us, together far longer than you have been around! I don't mind people stating opinions, but you are going too far. Aleshia is part of the key to our freedom. I know it. Now trust me on this and get everyone ready. I will not lose anyone, nor will we leave anyone behind. If we must leave equipment, then we will. Am I clear?"

"Crystal," Galina sneered.

"Good now do as I say. I will go talk with Leon. I am going to need you both to coordinate the evac. We have enough vehicles, but it will be tight. The clock is ticking so please get a move on."

"All right, all right, I am going." Galina said and started walking, then paused at the doorway. "And Deven, I am sorry. I know what you have done for us all, it is just ... well ..."

"Don't worry about it. We are all under tremendous pressure. Just don't lose sight of the goal. We all have the same goal, and together we will achieve it."

Galina smiled. "Yes we will." She said as she disappeared around the corner.

Deven found Leon working on the holographic generator. "Hey Deven, I think I found a way to reduce the energy requirements by half, if we can–"

"Never mind that. Mechands are going to be here in less than an hour."

"What! How? Are you certain they are coming here and not just flying over like they usually do?"

Deven shook his head and sighed. "Yes I am sure. Galina is

going to coordinate the evac and while we do have enough vehicles for everyone, it is going to be tight. I told her I wanted everyone gone before the Mechands get here. But I do not think that is feasible. I am wondering if you could buy us some time?"

"What did you have in mind?"

"Could you repurpose the holofield to something more solid?"

Leon nodded. "Sure I can make it feel like someone is hitting a brick wall instead of passing right through. Takes more than three times the power though, which is why we never did it."

"Do you think we have enough to pull it off?"

"Just, it will be dodgy. But if we shut down a few things, sure. Not sure how long I can keep it at full power, but it would certainly be a surprise to anyone trying to go through it."

"Can you boost it a little more so that it incarcerates anything that touches it?"

Leon nodded. "If I take all the power we got, sure. But we risk blowing the whole thing with an overload."

Deven smiled. "And how long would the overload take?"

Leon grinned. "I think I know what you have in mind."

"Oh really? Since when did you start to be a mind reader?"

Leon laughed. "Well I have been around you long enough haven't I? Anyway, yes the overload would take a little bit to build. Probably ten minutes. But when it goes, it will take everything here with it."

"Is there any way to stop it once it starts?"

"Heck no, and you probably already figured that."

"I did, but had to be sure. Leon, I will not give this facility to the Mechands. They have taken too much of our civilization as it is."

"You will not get any argument from me on that score. And before you ask, I can have the changes ready in about twenty minutes. Just let me know when to flip the switch."

"That will be my job. After you set it up, I want you helping Galina. You just tell me which one to flip."

Leon shook his head. "No way, what happens if something goes wrong. Then what?"

"I will just have to make sure nothing does. Don't worry about it. I need you helping Galina."

"All right, all right, I will help her. By the way where are we going?"

"The beta site."

Leon choked. "You're kidding! It is not ready yet!"

"It is ready enough, I just got a report. It will be rough, but we will make do. And I will need you to grab what equipment we can to help."

"I will do what I can Deven, you know that. Let me get to work on this and I will go help Galina."

"I know you will, let me know when it is done." Deven said as he headed out of the building.

"Right." Leon said his fingers already deep in a mass of wires.

Deven found Aleshia right where he hoped, in the quarters they had given her. He knocked on the door.

"Who is it?" Aleshia called from behind the door.

"It's Deven."

"Oh sure come on in."

Deven opened the door and found her in a plain black pair of pants and a conforming green shirt with a scoop neck. He almost hoped she was still wearing the same dress he first saw her in. "We need to talk."

"Oh we do? I thought we had already done a lot of that. And why are you visiting personally this time? Got tired of being in my mind?"

Deven chuckled. "Hardly, but–" He started to say just as the alarms went off throughout the facility.

Aleshia's eyes widened. "What is that?"

"That is why I wanted to talk to you. Mechands are on their way and will be here soon."

"Mechands! How did they find this place? I know I never would have."

Deven sighed. "They had help."

"Help? Who here would help them?"

"Well not willingly. It was your car, I didn't think they would have placed a tracker on it yet. I was wrong."

Aleshia's eyes widened further. "My car? That means I brought them right to you! I am so sorry! I had no idea!"

"I know you didn't, and neither did I. And as you probably guessed we need to leave soon, so pack your things. It looks like you have a few." He said looking around the room. A few items of makeup, combs, and a fresh toothbrush sat on the counter. On the floor several shirts, pants, and shoes rested in an open general issue bag.

"Yes Galina was nice enough to give me a few things." She said with a smile.

"Good, pack them up and put them in your car."

"My car? Is that safe? Won't they just track me wherever I go? And what about everyone else?"

"Galina found the tracker and removed it, no one can follow you now. As for everyone else, we have enough vehicles, but it will be tight. That is why I want to use yours."

Aleshia nodded. "Sure no problem. It is not the fastest out there, but I hope fast enough."

"It will be fine. Pack up, and wait at your car. I will join you there as soon as I can." Deven said leaning forward to hug her, then held back. "I will see you soon." He smiled and headed out the door.

A few moments later with a data tab in hand he found Leon closing the last panel on the large holo projector's main console. "Is it done?"

Leon nodded. "It is done. I rigged it into the main power systems." He said pointing to a large round coiled device bolted on to the side. "Flip the switch on this booster and three seconds later it will have full power. Ten minutes after that, everything goes up in smoke."

"How long with the shield itself last?"

"Depends on what they throw at it."

Deven consulted his data tab and frowned. "Looks like 2 *Carbonia* carriers and several smaller ships with it."

"*Carbonia* carriers!? They are not fooling around. Wow, I have only seen one for a second, and I don't think anyone else here ever has."

"Yes their main guns are formidable, and people think they are to defend against meteorites that make it through the mesosphere? I never could understand how people bought into that one."

Leon snorted. "Me either. But they do. Probably because they feel the Mechands only serve us, instead of the other way around."

Deven carefully looked at the booster. "This is a capacitor booster right?"

"Yep, builds power by cycling it through the various crystals causing a resonance that amplifies the power greatly.

But only for a short period. If left unchecked, well you know what happens."

Deven turned towards Leon. "Leon, what would happen if I waited about five minutes and initiated an energy purge on the booster?"

"Well the raw power would feed back into the main holo projector."

"And then?"

"Well in theory ..." Leon's eyes brightened. "That's brilliant! It would shoot a beam directly up incinerating anything in its path."

"And then?"

"Well that much power blasting out of the dish would kill the projection instantly, and five minutes after that, everything here goes up in smoke. As I said once the process starts, there is no stopping the reaction inside the main power cells."

Deven grinned. "I thought so. Go help Galina with the evac, I will take care of this. They will be here soon." Deven consulted his data tab, he saw the large Mechand ships getting closer every second. "Probably in 10 minutes or less."

"Gotcha." Leon said as he ran out of the building.

Deven checked his data tab again, ran a few simulations, and silently prayed this worked. Five minutes later, he engaged the booster. Immediately raw power flowed into it, then back into the main power cells. A second later every light in the building began to flash red and a voice came over the speakers. "Danger! Main system in overload, estimate total failure in ten minutes. All personnel must evacuate immediately!"

6

Aleshia wandered the streets engulfed in a blur of activity. She had already packed everything in her car. But hated feeling like a fifth wheel. So much to do and she wanted to help. "I know Deven told me to wait in the car, but I just can't sit there," she muttered to herself.

She saw Leon running down the street. "Hey Leon!"

He stopped at the sound of her voice, looked around, then ran over. "Hi Aleshia, I assume you know the Mechands are coming?"

"Yeah Deven told me, look I am really sorry. It is because of me you are in this mess."

Leon smiled and grabbed her shoulder. "Hey don't worry, it would have happened sooner or later. You just sped up the time-table a bit. But hey, it will be worth when you help us rid the world of them forever."

"Me? What can I do?"

"Uh, never mind. I meant help us, with all of us together we can't lose. Right?" He gave her a lopsided grin.

"Yes I suppose. But it sure don't see like it at the moment."

"I know. Excuse me but I have to run, we don't have much time left before they are here." He said heading off in his original direction when Aleshia called out.

"One thing!"

He ran back. "Yes?"

"Can I help?"

"I think we have it covered. Evac plans have been on the books since we first came here. Don't worry it will be fine. Did Deven tell you to do anything?"

"Yes, wait in my car."

"Then I would say the best way to help is to do as he said." Leon said as he ran off again.

"Where is he? Do you know?" she shouted after him.

"He is in the holo projector!" He shouted back not even slowing down as he ducked into a side building.

Aleshia wondered where that was, then remembered that it would have to be the large dish shaped building at the other end of the street. She immediately ran towards it. A moment later she found Deven inside looking intently at his data tab. All the screens were flashing red warnings with a count down clock clearly visible on one of them. "Deven?" she said breathing hard. "What is going on?"

"Aleshia! What are you doing here? Didn't I tell you to wait in the car?"

"Yes but I feel useless, I want to help. After all, it is because of me you have to leave."

Deven shook his head. "No it wasn't your fault. Not at all. Get that out of your head right now. I could have chose to bring you in differently. The mistake was mine, not yours. Okay? Besides, you will help us in ways you can't imagine."

Aleshia blinked. "What do you mean?"

"Never mind, now will you please go wait in the car? I will see you there shortly."

"I want to stay and–"

A loud voice came over the building's speakers. "Danger!

Five minutes until total overload of primary power systems. All personnel must evacuate the area immediately!"

"Whaaaat!?" Aleshia screamed.

Deven consulted his data tab and brought up a full scan. The Mechands were close enough to risk the high power scan being detected now. The two large cruisers were almost on top of them. One was holding back, but the other was approaching fast. Checking the details he could see why. Intensive scans directed precisely at their location. No doubt they knew exactly where to go and have determined the ice and snow they were seeing was a just hologram. "They are about to get a large surprise," Deven muttered.

"Who is?"

"The Mechands. Here I will show you." He said as he engaged an outside camera feed display on his data tab. Aleshia looked over to see a lot of ice and snow, and a very large ship descending fast, oblivious to the image below them. A moment later the ship touched the image of the ground. Instantly, a large explosion occurred along its vertical engines and spread to other parts of the ship. Fire belched out of every corner as a chain reaction occurred growing in intensity with each explosion. Until nothing was left and the carrier simply evaporated as though it had never been. "Okay scratch one Mechand ship."

Aleshia blinked. "How in the world–"

"I might have had the idea, but it was Leon's genius that made it possible. He turned the hologram into one heavy hitting force field. Unfortunately it won't be able to do that a second time. But I have another surprise for the second one." Then, as Leon predicted, the hologram's matrix couldn't take the extra power feedback and dissolved revealing the large ship hovering directly above the complex.

Aleshia pointed to one of the monitors and the large ship now approaching fast. "Deven I think we had better go now."

"Just a minute, I need to let the power build back a bit more."

"Build back for what? That is the biggest ship I have ever seen! I never knew Mechands had such large ships! How are we going to beat that without the shield you made?"

"Technically they are only supposed to be used to protect us from meteorites from landing. Well you can see how that is an outright lie. But I have one more trick up my sleeve. Don't worry," he said grinning.

Several ships were about ready to leave, and Deven knew if they did, they would be blasted out of the sky. Sighing heavily, he looked towards Aleshia. "Aleshia take my hand."

Aleshia blinked and took a step back. "Seems a bit premature don't you think?"

"Please, just do it, and close your eyes."

"All right." She said stepping forward, taking his hand, and closing her eyes.

Deven focused his mind. *Everyone. Please listen to me. Do not leave right now. Wait another minute. You will know when. Then meet at the beta site.* Deven opened his eyes and staggered a bit with the drain. Aleshia also took a step back feeling rather worn out.

"What the heck was that!" She said rubbing her temples shaking a dizzy feeling from her mind.

"Your abilities are very unique, but weak. Together we were able to send everyone in range a message. While I could have done it myself, the drain would have knocked me out for a bit."

Aleshia looked at him dumbfounded.

"And don't bother I know what you are going to say. Sorry

I didn't tell you sooner, there just wasn't time. And yes I can read your mind right now, a side effect of our link. I had to lower all my defenses, it will fade in a minute."

Aleshia looked at him, uncertain of her feelings. This man just used her, but by the same token cared a great deal for her. She felt an odd twinge to just trust him, for now. "All right, I hope it does. I don't want you reading my every thought."

Deven laughed. "Soon you will be able to block me if you want. I will show you how." He looked back at his data tab and the outside feed. The large Mechand ship approached much slower than the first. No doubt trying to deduce what had happened. Finally it reached the center of the complex, and right over the holo projector. "Gotcha!" He muttered while pressing a large button on the booster.

The holo projector building shook as raw power flowed into the dish. Building exponentially until a large beam shot up out of the center and hit the Mechand ship head-on, blasting right through the middle section. Time seemed to stand still as the beam rapidly increased in size until it was the full size of the building. The ship hovered helplessly as if speared through the heart. Then the beam grew in size again into a full conical blast that totally engulfed the ship. Fire buried from the inside out in an ever expanding plume of destruction until it disintegrated as though it never existed.

"Wow." Aleshia muttered under her breath.

The building shook again but this time for a different reason. The automated voice boomed over the speakers. "Warning! This facility will overload in two minutes! All personnel must evacuate immediately!"

Deven grabbed Aleshia's hand. "Time to go!" He said pulling her out of the building and towards her car. The projector dish shook again, which reverberated out to the other buildings. Signs and porches began to fall off. Glass windows exploded under the strain.

Aleshia looked up and saw different cars, large heavy lifting construction vehicles, and cargo haulers ascend into the sky and disappear like fireflies into the night as they engaged their overdrives.   The ground's ever-increasing movement made it impossible to run by the time they reached Aleshia's car.

Deven hopped into the drivers seat. "I'm driving." But the car refused to power on.

Aleshia pulled him out of the seat. "No I am! The car is keyed to me, get in!" She shouted pushing a button that popped the passenger door open as a building fell behind them.

"Okay, you don't have to tell me twice!" He said hopping into the passenger side while she fired up the engine. A moment later they were hovering up out of the complex. "Um I don't mean to be pushy, but can this thing go any faster?"

"It is safer if I let the engine warm up a little before I apply full thrust."

"Look in a few seconds, if we are not away from here, we won't have to worry about anything ever again!"

Aleshia's eyes widened. "You mean ... wait a sec how big of a blast is that thing going to put out?"

"I don't know, and I don't want to be anywhere around to find out okay? So PUNCH IT!"

Aleshia hit the overdrive dialing it to maximum. They were slammed back into their seats with the sudden acceleration as the holo projector reached critical mass. The large dish shuddered and folded in upon itself, then exploded in an ever growing fireball. Microseconds later it engulfed the entire complex and continued to expand. Fire lashed out at them and melted a tail light before they were out of range. Red hot lava broke through the surface incinerating anything not already blasted and burnt beyond recognition. Several large jets of lava shot up over two thousand feet into the sky with the pressure fully released, then came back to earth as large solidified rock. A new volcano was born.

7

"Wow." Aleshia said under her breath looking out the windows at the newly made volcano as they continued speeding away. "Was that really necessary?"

Deven sighed. "Yes, I am sorry to say it was."

"Why? You destroyed the two ships."

"And they have more, and will be back here in force. That is why we couldn't leave anything for them to find. I hated to destroy it all, but there was little choice. It's a good thing they didn't bother launching fighters. If they did, I doubt we would have got away so easily."

Aleshia looked at the rapidly brightening horizon as night gave way to dawn. "And I bet they won't fall for that same trick twice."

"Yes, you are correct. I am surprised we were able to take out both ships. I am also fairly certain at our next encounter, they will have more ships. I think we used up our one 'easy' card, if we ever had one."

Aleshia nodded. "Now where are we going?"

"Our beta site. I hadn't anticipated moving there for some time, but the main facilities should be operational. It will be a bit rough, but we will manage."

"Beta site? Where is it?"

Deven grinned. "Somewhere even more remote than Iceland."

"More remote? Where is it? The North Pole."

"Well you are partly right. It is a pole, but the other side."

Aleshia glared at him. "It's in Antarctica?"

"Yes."

"And doesn't Antarctica have a bad storm that is almost the size of the entire content, has raged for the past three years, and everyone is to avoid it at all costs?"

"Yes there is a bit of a storm going on there. But not as bad as has been reported." Deven said glancing out the window.

Aleshia looked directly at him. "Are you insane?"

Deven turned his head. "Well some might say I am. But think about it, no one is going to go there, and that includes Mechands."

"I don't know if my car can navigate such a storm. I am not sure if I even want to try."

"Look, I know a path that will get us to the beta site. The corridor, as we call it, it is a location where the storm is mostly held at bay due to the large ice formations."

"Are you sure?"

Deven smiled. "Trust me."

Aleshia's mind whirled, here a man that she had barely met, yet was asking her to trust him with her life. Her head immediately said no, her heart felt something different though. A tugging, but something more. And he had just saved her from the Mechands. "All right, for the moment."

"Good, that is all I ask. Until I can prove I am worthy of that trust. Now just head towards the most eastern edge of Antarctica," he said keying in a set of navigation coordinates, "once there I can guide you further."

Aleshia nodded. "Okay. And one more question."

"Yes?"

"What was that thing where you held my hand and spoke to everyone?"

"I am sorry about that, I really am. I didn't want to, but I was afraid anything else would have been overheard by the Mechands, or worse someone might have missed the message."

"You didn't answer my question. What was it?"

Deven sighed. "It was a link. A linking of minds. Mine and yours. It wasn't a full link, but it was enough."

"But why did you want to?"

"As I said, I could have done it without you, but then it would have caused me to pass out. Or at least freeze me for a few minutes, time we didn't have. With your help, the draining effect was easily mitigated."

Aleshia nodded. "I can't believe I was able to help you. I didn't think these abilities I had were that strong."

Deven grinned. "They aren't ... yet. But it was enough to help me. Don't worry they will grow."

Aleshia sighed. "That is what I am afraid of."

The rest of the trip they sat in silence. Roughly two hours later they exited overdrive off the coast of Antarctica. Winds were already kicking up even at this distance. "Okay," Deven said pointing, "down there you should see a depressed area heading into the interior."

"I do," Aleshia said nodding, "it looks only a few feet wider than my car. Does that lead the whole way?"

"No, it forks off into several other directions at various intervals. Almost like a maze but not quite. Still, it is possible to get lost in there for some time."

"And I hope you know the way."

"I do. Whenever you are ready."

Aleshia smiled. "I am, brace yourself, we are going in." She said lowering the car to a few inches above the icy ground and gently eased into the corridor. Deven was right, the ice formations on either side blocked most of the wind. She depressed the accelerator and their speed increased. The formations moved past at a faster rate, but not enough to preclude stopping instantly should she need to.

It was beautiful. The ice glinted with sunlight for the first part. But by the time they reached one of the turns, the sky had turned dark grey, and the wind howled just a few meters above them. Aleshia shivered at the sound and had to turn on her headlights.

"Listen to that," she said still shivering.

"Yes, we are in the middle of the storm. Whatever you do, don't go out of the corridor. I doubt we would survive, let alone get back in."

"Don't worry about that. I am not leaving these ice walls. How much farther?"

"Oh a few more miles. Just don't get complacent, these ice formations can be deceptive. You think it is some distance ahead, then it is right in front of you. The long distance makes it difficult. And before you ask, Auto-Nav doesn't work here. The system doesn't have the skyway beacons, or the other usual indicators. It will just run us into a wall."

"Actually I wasn't planning on it. I felt it was too tricky in here to trust the Auto-Nav."

Deven grinned. "Smart girl."

Aleshia smiled back. "I try."

After many miles and a blur of turns later they floated into a dead end. "Umm I think you made a mistake," Aleshia said pointing, "there is nothing here."

"Yes there is. Just land."

"Here?"

"Yes right here."

"Now I know you are insane. There is nothing here!"

Deven smiled. "I thought you said you were going to trust me? The area right below us is flat. It won't hurt your car. Just land okay?"

"Okay, but I still think you are insane." She said as the car slowly lowered onto the ice covered bottom of the corridor. They sat there for several minutes before Aleshia looked Deven straight into the eye. "Well?"

A second later they felt a jolt and the ice formations started growing. Aleshia looked around, and realized the formations weren't growing, they were being lowered. A moment later the headlights glinted off metal ahead of them as they continued to descend. After what seemed like two buildings deep, they stopped. Aleshia's sat with her mouth open, at a loss for words.

There in front of them sat what looked like a giant ship hidden deep under the ice. Landing pads on its top face were clearly visible on the large flat surface. Off to the one side a large tower that extended high above the landing area, that she assumed, was the bridge. Several large energy cannons were studded throughout and concentrating at each corner of the roughly rectangular ship. Hover units of immense size hung off at various locations. But the largest were in the back and under the middle section. Lights above it illuminated the whole expanse. Many of the vehicles she saw earlier were either parked up on its generous landing surface or down below on the ice.

"Okay what is that?!" Aleshia said pointing.

"Why that is the beta site as I told you."

"Beta site my foot! That is a warship! Something like the

old history files talk about. And they existed long before the Mechands."

Deven smiled. "I had no idea you were so astute on our history. Yes you are quite correct. It is a warship from long ago, she is called the *Defiant*. Apparently lost here in the Antarctic during one of the large storms that now ravage this land. But we are not certain. Repairing her engines and other main systems have been the priority, not the recovery of her damaged log files.

"And how did you find this?"

"We were searching for a location that the Mechands were unlikely to find. First we found the corridor, and while exploring it, Otis got a ping of something huge in the ice. Obviously the ice and storms had kept it from being discovered. Or the Mechands didn't care. Either way, she is something that can help us."

"Is she operational?"

"Mostly. The engines are online, or should be. We haven't actually tested them yet. Many of the computer systems haven't been updated either. And she is a bit rough on the inside. We didn't plan on moving in for a while."

"Wow I am impressed. Okay so where do I land?"

Deven pointed to the top deck. "Just pick an open space on the deck. Don't worry it will be fine, she is stable."

The moment they touched down Leon ran out to greet them. "Deven! Good to see you. I see our little *surprise* worked well. Better than we hoped in fact."

"Yes it did. And it should have bought us some time. They don't know how many of us escaped, if any."

"Yep. Well I have to get back down to the engine room. I will give you a full report later."

Deven cocked an eyebrow. "I thought they were online?"

"Well, umm, yeah they are. They just need a little love. Don't worry they will be ready when you need them." He said running off below deck.

Aleshia leaned over to Deven. "Why do I have my doubts about that?"

"Hey, Leon knows engines better than anyone. If he says they will work, they will."

"Uh-huh," Aleshia grunted.

"Don't worry, we will be ready soon enough." He said walking over to the hatch heading below deck. Galina popped her head up through the hatch before he could enter.

"Oh good you are here! I have some questions for you."

Deven sighed. "Already? I haven't even got below deck yet."

Galina laughed. "Yes already. Do you want most of the people in the upper or lower decks?"

"I thought that was already assigned?"

"Well it was, were using the same method the original ship had. But now that I thought about it, we have a couple of options. We don't have enough people to fill the *Defiant* like she was back in the day, so we can afford to do things differently."

"Well other than the top cabins, which I think we already reserved, I will let everyone choose their own. But I do prefer everyone be close to the center structure if possible. That should give them the best protection, should we need it."

Galina nodded. "Yes I agree," she said checking her data tab, "Leon is working on the engines, they should be online soon. Power generation is online. We are continuing to update the computer systems but it is slow going. This ship just wasn't designed for much of our equipment."

"I know, but we will have to make do. I am sure if anything gives us problems, Leon can whip it into shape."

"Probably, but I would feel a lot better if everything worked as it should."

"Wouldn't we all! If it was my choice, you would have all the latest equipment and more of it than we need."

"Wouldn't that be nice. But I know we have to make do with what we have. Don't worry everything will be operational soon. The place is a bit of a mess, but that wasn't our priority as you know."

"Yes I know." Deven nodded. "Do you have a cabin ready for Aleshia?"

"Nope, but she can pick out anyone she likes. Unless it is already taken that is."

"And I assume I have the old captain's cabin?"

Galina nodded. "Yes, I took the liberty of putting your items we grabbed during the evac in your cabin. I think we got it all. I didn't have time to double-check."

"Thank you. Has anyone had any sleep yet?"

Galina shook her head. "Nope, we really wanted to make this place our home as much as possible before we did."

"Well if the power generator is online, then we can afford to rest. The Mechands won't follow us. Or at least not until we are ready, so everyone can get some sleep. I don't want mistakes made because people are too tired."

"All right, I will let everyone know to get some rest."

"Well not everyone, I think we should leave some people out keeping an eye on the systems, such as they are. Especially the power generator."

Galina laughed. "Do you really think I wouldn't have someone watching that? HA! At this point it is the least trusted system on the ship. Well at least in my book. Leon says it is fine, but still I have my doubts."

"If Leon says it is fine, then it is. But have someone watching it, nonetheless."

"You got it."

"Good. I'm going to show Aleshia around, then get some rest."

"Will do. I will get you if anything comes up." Galina said as she disappeared down the hall below deck.

Deven snorted. "Of that I have no doubt."

Aleshia followed Deven below. It was warmer, but not as nice as Iceland. "Brrr, it is cold in here."

"It will be warmer soon. We haven't brought the heating units up to full power yet. But the cabins should be better."

He showed her the engine room which didn't look near as bad as she feared. After stepping through tons of wiring, dust, junk, and other assorted debris, she thought the engines must be in even worse shape. But they actually looked to be in very good condition. The large central turbines encased in giant brackets glowed strongly even in their off condition. Leon was busy working when Deven approached.

"Leon! Shouldn't you be resting? I told Galina to pass on that we all need rest, especially after what just happened."

"Hey Deven, sure she did. But I am on the hunt of why this engine doesn't want to fire up. I am almost there, I can feel it. I couldn't sleep, anyway."

Deven shook his head. "Leon, could you please just go try? I don't want everyone dead on their feet. I know we have a lot to do here, but it can wait for now."

"Perhaps. All right, I will try to get some sleep, but if I can't I will just come back here deal?"

"That is all I ask, that you at least try."

"Thanks." Leon said heading out of the engine room when he stopped. His eyes lit up, and he turned back to the main console keying something in.

"Leon? Thought you were going to–"

"Just a sec! I had an idea!" He said leaning over the console. He punched in something and a schematic appeared. Smiling he keyed in a command and hit commit. With a giant grunt the one turbine began to power up. Then it kick-started another, then another. The room became alive with power as all the different parts came online. Sparks shot between several open panels. Levels increased slowly then Leon hit one last key. Power shot to the limits and the giant ship grunted as it freed itself from the ice below to hover an inch above the cave floor. "There we go!"

"Leon! You did it!"

Leon grinned. "Did you ever have any doubt? The *Defiant* can fly now. She still needs work before we want to take her out for a spin, but she can stand on her own two feet now. Sort of speak." He said while carefully lowering her back to rest on the ice floor and shut down the massive engines.

"Thank you Leon."

"You are welcome, and now I think I will go sleep a bit." He yawned and headed out of the engine room and down the hallway.

"I have never seen anything quite like that." Aleshia said after Leon was out of earshot.

"Heh, I doubt anyone has for a long time. Ships like this were taken out of service and dismantled long ago."

Deven showed her the rest of the ship. The medical center, bridge, and most other areas were still in disrepair. But as promised, the crew cabins and mess hall were in relatively good shape. Reaching the captain's cabin, Deven found two large boxes on the floor with a keypad on the top. He keyed in his access and found all of his data tabs, clothes, and personal items were there. He made a mental note to thank Galina later for doing that. The woman was a wonder.

"Captain's cabin eh?" Aleshia said from behind leaning on the door frame, "so does this make you Captain Deven?"

Deven laughed. "No, I never liked fancy titles. There is no need for one anyway, everyone here knows who I am. Did you find a cabin you like?"

"They all look the same, so I just picked one two doors down from yours. I hope that is okay."

"Well you heard Galina, if it wasn't occupied, it is yours."

"It wasn't. I grabbed my stuff from the car, and I am going to get some sleep. I hope you do the same. You look like you could really use it."

"I wish I could, way too much to do."

"Aht aht aht," Aleshia said waiving her finger, "you told Galina everyone had to rest. That includes you."

Deven laughed. "No it doesn't."

"I think Galina would disagree. So would everyone else here. None of us want you yawning all the time, or asleep on your feet."

"I am not that bad."

"The bags under your eyes say otherwise."

"Really? Do I look that tired?"

Aleshia nodded. "You do. Now are you going to get some sleep or do I have to get everyone in here to enforce it?"

Deven grinned. "Why do I get the feeling I don't have a choice in this?"

Aleshia grinned back. "Oh I don't know, perhaps because, you *don't?*"

"All right, all right, I will sleep. Right after I check these–"

"No, right now." Aleshia said as she took a data tab out of Deven's hand and sat it on the desk. "If I have to get some sleep, and believe me I would much rather poke around, you are going to do the same."

Deven laughed. "Okay, you got me. Right now. I won't even look at these reports."

"Good." Aleshia said as she started closing the door. "Sleep well."

— 8 —

Aleshia awoke to pounding above her. Her eyes fluttered open, and she groaned. "Miles what is that sound?" She shouted before her eyes had a chance to focus. Miles was not here, and she would likely never see him again. He was a Mechand, and helped the Nexus track her down the first time.

Aleshia shook her head to clear it and shivered as a chill ran through her. The air was still cold. While she managed to find an extra portable heating unit, hours later it still hadn't warmed up the room. Of course, it had been a long time since this room had seen heat, so it wasn't unexpected. She quickly dressed into a pair of green cargo pants and a black shirt. Sighing at the less-than-attractive look it gave her figure, she slipped on a black insulated jacket and went to see what all the pounding was about.

A deck above she found several men adding supports and welding them in place. "What is all this about?"

One of the men looked up from his welding and flipped back the dark goggles. "Oh sorry, Aleshia isn't it? I am Gregory, Deven told us we needed to reinforce this section as soon as possible."

"What for?"

"I think he plans on taking off tomorrow."

"How? We are buried under the ice!"

"Hey, I don't know," Gregory shrugged, "he didn't have time to tell us much."

Aleshia headed off towards Deven's cabin. She found him as usual looking over several data tabs. "Deven, Gregory said we are taking off tomorrow? Isn't that a bit premature? I mean I don't know that much about the *Defiant*, but she doesn't exactly look like she could take off."

Deven looked up. "Why not?"

"Well for one thing she is buried under a lot of ice. For another, did you forget about the storm that is raging just above us?"

Deven smiled. "Don't worry about that. I have it all worked out. Or at least Leon does."

Aleshia sat in one of the thinly padded chairs. "Care to tell me?"

Deven sat down the data tab. "Why do you want to know?"

"Well since I have come here, I really haven't been told that much about your plans, or what we are doing. I know I am on the run, as is everyone else. I also know that due to me, you had to leave your previous home. I think many people here resent me for that. And well I would just like to know what is going on. I feel I should have a right to know more about you, about the people that have helped me. Can you blame me?"

Deven sat back. "No I can't. All right, what do you want to know first?"

"Well how about you? Who are you?"

Deven laughed. "I thought that was obvious?"

"Well humor me."

"Okay, well you know I am pretty much the leader here,

and not something I wanted but rather fell into. I have been on the run since I was in my teens when my abilities started to manifest themselves. At the time I thought like you, that I was hearing things. Or that it wasn't anything of consequence. But I learned otherwise."

Aleshia leaned forward. "What happened?"

My parents reported my strange behavior. At first nothing seemed to come of it. Then I had the feeling of being watched. Tracked everywhere I went. Late one night I spotted a Mechand shadowing me. I had an intense fear of it. Which was strange considering I had grown up with them and taught to think of them as our friends. I managed to lose it. And after that, about six of them showed up at my parents house looking for me. That is when I knew something was amiss.

"I watched carefully and after they left I snuck back in, grabbed what I could without my parents seeing me, and took off. Not knowing where I would go. I kept hiding out in various transports. I would take anything, just to keep on the move. Usually in the cargo hold. Most people would have reported a runway, if they knew. At some point I found myself in Australia, well it used to be called that."

Aleshia's eyes widened. "Australia?"

Deven nodded. "Australia. I met an old man named Fenton Vara that ran a small store and he took me in. Soon after the headaches increased and after each burst I found my abilities growing. At first just hearing surface thoughts. Then later on I could pull any information from someone's mind if I wanted. A few years later I found myself able to look inside machines. At first it was simple, something along the lines of sonar or radar. But that has grown over the past year. Still, it takes great concentration to use it for any length of time.

And the longer I use it, the more it drains me. My abilities sometimes show me the future. Usually in my dreams, and let me tell you, that still freaks me out at times."

Aleshia sat back. "And what do you want with me?"

Deven rocked in his chair slightly. "I don't want anything from you right now, only to take care of you. If you recall, you were being chased much as I was. Everyone here has their reasons. Some have mental abilities, others just want to help us out. Leon I have known the longest. His gift I think you have already seen: he is a technological wizard. I swear he could make a *Defiant* out of package sealing tape if he really wanted to."

Aleshia chuckled. "Yes from what I have seen, he probably could. But why did you try to visit me, rather than sending someone else? It seems like you would be more valuable here."

Deven stood up, walked over to the window, and gazed out at the large ice cavern the *Defiant* rested in. "Perhaps, but I hoped that if I did it myself, you would understand and not run. I thought that I knew you well enough and could set aside your fears. But as we both know, I failed miserably in that."

"It wasn't your fault. And I am sorry I didn't listen to you."

Deven turned to face her. "The failure was not yours. You had no reason to trust me. And I should have not assumed the trust would immediately go both ways. That was again my mistake." He sat back down in his padded chair which made a slight creak in complaint. "Anyway, that is not important. You are here now, and safe. The situation could have been far worse. And I am grateful. You mean a lot to me."

"I do? But we hardly know each other."

"Aleshia, as I said I have felt you for a long time. My

mind found yours long before you could respond. Of course I didn't know where you were until your abilities asserted themselves. And they will continue to grow. You have no idea yet, but I will teach you," he said with a smile. "That is if you will trust me."

Aleshia smiled. "I do trust you."

"Good, and I promise I will never do something without your permission."

Aleshia smirked. "Of that I am sure." She said with a bit of 'just try it buddy' attitude in her voice. "One more question, everyone is working hard on getting this ship operational. But how are we going to leave? I mean we are deep beneath the ice and snow."

"Good question, and in short the *Defiant* has shields. When we activate them and power the main drive, we should be able to push our way up and through. Leon is working on that."

Just then Leon ran into the room. "Hey speak of the devil." Deven looked at the expression on Leon's face and instantly grew concerned. "What's wrong?"

"We have a big problem. I am not sure why, but the ice shelf above is starting to collapse. I estimate we have about two hours before really big chunks start to fall."

Deven got to his feet. "Okay move all the vehicles into the hangers. That will protect them as the hull is reinforced. But I am sure we can't withstand the full shelf collapsing."

Leon shook his head. "Nope it would be like an egg supporting a car."

"How long until the shields are operational?"

"Probably 12 hours."

Deven sighed. "Is there anyway to slow the collapse and give us more time?"

Leon rubbed his chin. "Hmm, if we use one of the main guns to surgically remove the ice at key points, that would reduce the stress and reinforce the overall structure at the same time."

Aleshia looked at Leon. "How?"

Leon smiled. "Simple engineering, it will redistribute the weight shifting it from the center of the cavern to the edges and the walls. It won't hold long-term. But it would be enough to give us the 12 hours to get the shields online."

"Okay try it. We don't have much to lose."

"Unless the whole thing falls in." Aleshia sighed under her breath.

"Deven I will need your help to target the locations."

Deven cocked an eyebrow. "I thought your scanners would be better?"

"Normally yes, but this ice has an odd reflective quality. I might be off by a few inches, and the cuts need to be exact."

Deven nodded. "Okay, I will be there. How long until you are ready?"

"One of the guns is almost operational now. I can cannibalize a couple of parts from the others and have it going within the hour. I will also have to borrow one of the computer systems we have hooked into the propulsion system right now."

"Okay do it. And call me when you are ready."

An hour later Deven, Leon, and Galina were up on the bridge. Wires ran everywhere. Leon had got one of the cannons modified into a powerful pinpoint energy scalpel. "Okay Deven, ready when you are." Leon said leaning over the display and controls just below it.

Deven closed his eyes for a few moments. Sweat beaded on his forehead as his mind reached out. He pushed harder and could feel the ice. Then a little more. "Ahh I see." He said, then opened his eyes and staggered forward, rubbing his temples.

Aleshia ran over to him. "Deven?"

"I am okay, just drained me a bit." He walked over to Leon and pointed at his screen. "Along here and here should do it."

"Okay thanks. I was thinking a little over to the left. Glad I had you check."

Deven nodded. "Yes the ice shelf is deceptive. The weight is shifting just above what we can see, which is probably the reason for the instability."

Aleshia piped up. "But why is it in the first place? The *Defiant* has been here for a long time, why in the world is it falling in now?"

"I suspect it is due to our work in here. The temperature might be raising ever so slightly. Not enough to melt, but enough to cause cracking and undermine the stability." Leon said watching the monitor intently. "Deven, I am going to shoot a guide beam at the locations you said. Please check that I am on target. We can't afford a mistake."

"Okay," Deven said closing his eyes. "Ready when you are."

Leon activated the guide and a high intensity green beam shot out from the cannon striking a location on the ceiling. "Okay, how is that?"

Deven stood still with his eyes closed for several seconds. "A little to the left."

Leon adjusted the control stick to the left a tiny bit. "How is that?"

"Just a little more, then towards us a little. Perhaps two inches." Deven said never opening his eyes. Sweat actively pooled on his forehead then ran down. "There you got it. Activate the scalpel."

Leon nodded and pressed a button on his controls. The green beam cut off and immediately high intensity red beam shot out striking with pinpoint accuracy. "Okay and moving forward. Let me know when to stop." He said as the beam sliced along the indicated course.

"Okay cut the beam ... right ... about ... *now.*" Deven said and Leon shut it off in the same instant. A second later he turned the guidance beam back on and placed it at the second location.

"Deven, how is that?"

By now Deven gripped the side of a console for support. "To the right about two inches then forward one inch." Leon manipulated the controls, and the beam moved in quick succession. "Okay there. Start cutting moving away from us, I will tell you when to stop." Leon switched off the guide beam and turned on the scalpel again. The beam sliced into the ice with perfect precision. "Okay ... stop ... *now.*" A moment later a huge triangular section of the ice ceiling dropped hitting the ground two inches from the *Defiant.*

Deven started to fall backwards and Aleshia ran to steady him. "Are you okay?"

"Yes. I just need rest. That took a lot of out of me."

Leon checked his scanners. "You go rest. That seems to have given us the time we need to get the shields online. Don't worry, we can do it."

"Do you need help to get Deven back to his cabin?" Galina asked, "I really should help Leon."

Aleshia shook her head. "I can take care of him."

"Hmm? What was that?" Deven said still rubbing his

temples holding onto a console with one hand and Aleshia holding him up with the other.

Aleshia wrapped his arm around her shoulders. "Come on Deven, you need to go back to your cabin."

"Cabin? Yes I am a bit tired," he said groggily.

Aleshia led him down the various stairs going through deck after deck to finally arrive at his cabin. She pulled back the sheets on his bunk and pushed him into it. He mumbled "Thank you." And instantly fell asleep. She turned to leave when she felt a pull. A tug at her heart. She looked down at his sleeping face and smiled. In that moment she saw beneath the surface that everyone else saw, to his core. She saw the love he had for her, kept tightly hidden from view lest he should frighten her again.

She took his hand in hers and sat next to him. She had never felt anything like this before. And didn't know what to do. She closed her eyes and tried to go deeper still. Not really knowing what she was doing, she entered his mind.

There were images of her from long ago. Images that he had received in his mind but not knowing from whom or where. She followed the memories and saw that he fell in love with her when she was still with her parents. He had considered trying to find her, but didn't want to risk causing her problems. He felt the special link between them and couldn't bear to lose it. She saw his difficult life. His impossible parents. How he always tried to help people, and the many that took advantage of him. The years of being on the run until he met up with Fenton, finally finding a home at last. And yet never feeling complete.

Aleshia shook and in that instant she realized that Deven might be the one she had looked for all her life, her true soulmate. While he had been able to feel her in his mind. She had not been strong enough to do the same until now. She opened her eyes and let go of his hand breaking the mind-link. Then stood up, covered Deven with the blanket, and went back to her cabin. She had a lot to think about.

$$-9-$$

Aleshia lay on her bed in deep thought. What to do? Could she trust what she saw in Deven's mind? Could it possibly be true? Or could it have been something he projected into her mind? No, it had to be true, he was asleep. Unless his unconscious mind projected ... No, it couldn't have been that either. Her mind whirled around and around. In the end she was no closer to a decision than when she started.

She sat up and sighed, this was getting her nowhere. Her eyes flashed in thought and a smile slowly crept across her face. Perhaps Leon could shed some light on the situation. Heading off she eventually found him below installing a new, vastly smaller power plant. "Is that going to be enough?" Aleshia said leaning in the doorway.

Leon looked up. "Hmm? Oh you mean the power core? Sure, it is brand new and one of the latest designs. Heck, it could put out more power than this old ship could take. We will have to be careful or it might burn out some systems." He said as he continued to secure it in its new home, then ran cables from the old system to the new one. "It may be a bit of a bypass, but it will work. Did you want something?"

"Yes, how much do you know about Deven?"

Leon dropped the cable he was working with. "Umm what

do you want to know?"

"For starters how well do you know him?"

"Well enough that I trust him with my life if that is what you are asking. He has saved our backsides more times than I can count. Why do you ask?"

"I just saw something and I am trying to make sense of it."

"Why don't you just ask him?"

"I could, but I would rather just ask you."

"Okay what about?"

"Do you know about his childhood?"

"I know his abilities developed early, and he was on the run from the Mechands for a long time."

"Did he ever talk about some girl in his dreams?"

"Yes he did, he said that she ..." Leon's voice trailed off and his eyes widened. "He thinks that you are *her*? Did he say that?"

"No, I just, well, happened to look in his mind by accident and saw all these weird images and thoughts."

"Oh. I wouldn't worry about it then. You know a man's mind tends to wander a lot while he is sleeping. Heck if that was a crime I would be in deep trouble." He said chuckling and affixed the last of the power transfer cables to the new power core. "I am surprised that you were able to get in at all. I know others have tried, he usually keeps his mental barriers up at all times."

"Yes you are probably right. I am just being silly. Now that you mentioned the mental barriers, I doubt I was inside at all. My abilities are not exactly fully developed as you know."

Leon nodded. "Yes I agree. Well if you will excuse me, I need to head up to the bridge and test this system."

"Oh of course. Sorry I shouldn't have bothered you."

"It is no bother at all." He said heading out of the power room.

"Do you need any help?" Aleshia shouted down the hallway.

"Sure, keep an eye on the status panel on the side of the new core. I will call down and ask for an update."

"Call down?" She asked, but he was already gone. Alehisa walked over to the new core, stepping over the myriad of cables, and found the status panel on the other side. The indicator read offline, and she wondered what Leon was talking about. A moment later a blue-green glow started to emanate from its center section. Then there was a flash and the power core roared to life. The status panel flipped through various diagnostics and finally settling on a general status page. It looked like the core was generating 75% of maximum output.

"What is the power level?" Leon's voice crackled from a nearby speaker.

Aleshia walked over to it and toggled the VOX. "I thought these didn't work."

"Yeah, I just fixed them and forgot to tell everyone," Leon chuckled. "Did the core power up okay? What is the power level at?"

"Yes it seemed to power up fine. And the level is holding at 75%."

"Wonderful, I am seeing the same. I am going to try lowering it from here, see if it responds." Leon said and she could hear him punch several keys.

Aleshia watched as the power level decreased. "The power dropped to 35% is that okay?"

"Sure is. We don't need that much right now. And everything else on the status panel shows normal?"

"Yes."

"Wonderful, now we have full control from the bridge. Thanks Aleshia."

"Welcome." She said as the intercom clicked off.

Several hours later Deven awoke with a large headache. "Ow!" He said rubbing his forehead. "I hope I don't have to do that again for a while." He muttered as he sat up on the old military bed. Checking his watch, he swung his feet over, stood up, and made his way to the bridge. He found Leon, Aleshia, and Galina huddled around a console.

"I am sure it will work," Leon said pointing at his screen, "the *Defiant* can do it."

Galina shook her head. "And blow every system we have in the process."

"No it won't do that. The shields may have issues after. But I am certain they will last long enough."

"Long enough for what?" Deven asked as he stood in the doorway leaning on the hatch.

They all looked up at once. "Deven! Shouldn't you be resting? You look like death ran you over," Aleshia said.

"I have rested enough." He said still rubbing his forehead. "Now what is this you have in mind Leon?"

"It is crazy!" Galina exclaimed.

Deven raised his hand. "Galina, please."

Galina rolled her eyes as Leon began to speak. "Well I think I can get us out of this cavern. One way is to use the shields and push our way out."

Deven nodded. "Yes that is what we planned before."

"Yes but that was before the cavern had other ideas. The shields are not exactly at full strength yet, and it will take too long to get them there, the cavern will collapse by then. But I have another thought."

Deven raised an eyebrow. "Which is?"

"We phase out."

"We phase out?" Deven asked.

"Well as you know there has been a lot of research into the possibility of moving one object through another without any ill effects."

Deven nodded. "Yes and the scientists could never make it work."

"Well that is because they were having Mechands help them. And you know how they like to hold us back. I think I can implement a partial phase shift in our shields that will allow us to go right through."

"Partial phase shift? That doesn't sound too promising."

"Well it will be enough. I think the problem is they were trying to go for a full shift, which of course if you do that, you also disappear from this universe. That also takes an incredible amount of power."

"You think?"

"See Deven! Leon has lost his mind!" Galina exclaimed waving her arms in Leon's direction.

Deven raised his hand again. "Leon are you sure this will work?"

"About 95% percent sure."

"And the alternative is we get crushed by a giant ice shelf in a few hours?"

Leon nodded. "Yes, that sounds about right."

"Doesn't sound like we have much of a choice."

Galina threw up her hands. "You are both crazy."

"Galina, do you have a better idea?" Deven said walking towards them.

"Yes, we leave the *Defiant* and go somewhere else."

"Where? And we would have to leave so much behind."

"I don't know. We would find some place," Galina sighed.

"And then the Resistance is scattered all over? I don't think we will have much of a chance all on our own. Together we are much stronger."

"Well we can't be too strong if we are dead," Galina muttered.

"Galina, if you want to leave. You are welcome to. But I don't see that we have a choice. I won't break this group up. We don't have much left except this ship and ourselves. To lose either one right now, is not an option."

"I guess."

"Do you want to leave?"

"No. I will stay. I think Leon's craziness is starting to rub off on me." She said with a smirk.

"Good, then have Leon give you all that needs to be done and you can hand it out to everyone. We don't have a lot of time. Leon, how long before we can try?"

"If everyone hurries and we don't run into any problems, within the hour. I only need to make a slight modification to the shield emitters. If all the emitters are worked on at the same time, I know we can do it in the hour."

"Good, let's do this people. I have no intention of letting us get crushed one way or the other."

Fifty minutes later they all met back on the bridge. "Okay, I think we are ready." Leon said sitting back in his chair.

Galina blinked. "You think?"

"Okay, we are," Leon grinned.

"Hit it." Deven said as he reached for something to hold on to.

Leon nodded and activated the main drive. With a slight jerk the *Defiant* raised up several feet off of the cavern floor. "Engines are working perfectly. Shields going up ...*now*."

As he said it, a blue shimmer appeared around the *Defiant* encasing it in pure energy. Leon checked the systems. "Shields are working normally and approaching optimum phasing condition. Phasing in …5 …4 …3 …2 …1." Leon punched a button and the power core shot from 52% to over 85% power. The *Defiant* shook and vibrated.

"Is this normal?" Deven asked.

"No, but we should be okay. Just getting a little feedback. We are almost there. Just another few seconds." Leon said as the indicators finally reached 78.6% phase shift. "There! Engaging vertical. Hang on!" He said as he punched another button. With a groan the *Defiant* shot upwards at tremendous speed. Half a second later she passed through the cavern's ceiling. Everyone blinked as they saw ice passing through the roof and then through them. Two seconds later they were up above the ground but Leon didn't stop. "We need to get up above the storm, or it will tear us to shreds." He shouted as the wind howled through them.

Screens everywhere started flashing alerts. The main one on the wall flashed shield overload. "Dang it! Shields are overloading."

"Will they last?" Galina shouted.

"I hope so!" The *Defiant* shook more than ever before and several nearby consoles exploded. "Dang it! I just fixed those!" A moment later they finally emerged high in the air, well above the storm. But before Leon could shut down the shields, they did so by themselves with every emitter along the port side exploding under the strain. Leon quickly powered down the remaining emitters and lowered the power core output.

Deven looked around. "Status? Is everything stable?"

Leon hit several keys on his console. "Well the good news

is we are okay, and the *Defiant* is flying again."

Deven cocked an eyebrow. "And the bad news?"

"We blew out every shield emitter on the port side. I can try to compensate by moving half of the emitters from the starboard to port, but they will be much weaker."

"Well that is better than nothing. Do it as fast as you can. I don't like the idea of being caught with our shields down. I guess hold this position unless Mechands start to show up."

"Will do." Leon said as he looked over to Galina. "And you said it wouldn't work."

"I was wrong on that. But you are still crazy. Totally certifiable."

"Hey, sometimes that is the best kind." Leon said with a smirk.

Aleshia found Galina down below in one of the large landing bays handing out assignments to several people. "Oh Galina, great I have been looking for you."

"Oh? I didn't think I was that hard to find," Galina said laughing.

"Well, you are all over the *Defiant*, so yes it is at times."

"Okay, you have a point there. So what's up?"

"I was wondering if I could help in some way? I feel like the fifth wheel around here." She stopped to gesture around the large expanse that was fervently being restored.

"Hmm, well we are running low on food synth supplies, and if you could pick up a few new shield emitters that would be great."

"I would be happy to go get them. Just tell me where. I assume you don't just wander into any market."

Galina laughed. "No, I wish we could. There is a guy, Fenton Vara, he lives in a very remote section of what used to be called Australia. He funnels us supplies right under the Mechands scanners."

"But how? I thought the Nexus was plugged into all Mechands and everything was shared between them."

"Well he doesn't have a Mechand at all."

Aleshia's eyes widened. "Wow, that *is* unusual."

"Yes and thankfully he does, or we would really be in a fix. Anyway if you like I can pass you the coordinates. Your car's cargo area should be sufficient to carry enough concentrated material to last us a couple of months. Be aware though, it is heavy stuff." She said handing a card over to Aleshia.

Aleshia shrugged. "Sure, what isn't when concentrated like that. I will head right out." She took the data storage card and slipped it into her pocket. "Thanks. And the *Defiant* will be here when I get back?"

"You're welcome, and yes we will be here. We are in a stable hover. No reason to move at this point. But if you need to contact us, there is a encrypted link loaded on the card that your car's communication system can use."

Aleshia nodded as she headed up to her car. The deck had been cleared, with most of the different vehicles stored down inside the *Defiant's* hanger bays. The air whipped at her simple blue pants and jacket. Silently she thought about getting another set of clothes at this store, but then decided against it. Her ration credits would be instantly traced and the Resistance would lose a greatly needed contact.

She sighed climbing into the car and inserted the data card into the car's navigation slot. The screen lit up with "Coordinates Accepted. Engage Y/N?" She keyed in yes and the car took off for the content that used to be known as Australia.

About an hour later a call came in on her car's communication system. She raised an eyebrow. "That is odd, no one should be able to call me. I blocked everyone I knew." She muttered as the screen flipped on to reveal lines of static that slowly resolved into Miles' domed head.

"Hello Miss Aleshia." His voice came through calm and

soothing as always.

"Miles! How are you doing this?"

"I took the liberty of installing a communication override some time ago. Just in case."

"Don't call me again!" She said reaching for the cut off.

"Wait! Can we please meet? It is very important."

"I bet it is." Aleshia grunted under her breath. "No, that would not be wise. Goodbye Miles." She said flipping the switch to shut off the power to the system until she could get the override removed.

Thirty minutes later she reached the location Galina gave her. But the only thing in sight was a small little building that looked almost like a shack. Looking closer she noticed a large sign on the one side saying "Food, Gas, and More!". On the other side she saw the landing pad. She circled several times and an old man came out to waving. Finding nothing else but him on the scanner for many miles, she landed.

The man ran over to her. "G'day, I am Fenton, welcome to my place. What would you like?"

Aleshia eyed him warily as she flipped up the door leaving it pointing towards the sky. "Umm I came for a pick up. Galina said you could help me?"

Fenton's eyes brightened. "Ohhhh so she sent you did she? Well sure I have it all ready inside. Would you like to come in? It is awful hot out here. I have cold ice-cold beer inside, or would you prefer tea?"

Aleshia nodded. "Yes I would like an ice tea, thank you." She said getting out of the car.

Inside she found a quaint little store that only held a few small rows of items. "Wow," she said looking around, "I expected you had more in here."

Fenton smiled as he handed her an ice tea. "Ah but I do. Sit over on that chair please and hold on."

Aleshia sat in one of the two chairs set around a simple table. "I don't see what is so special about this chair that I have to hold on."

Fenton grinned. "You will." He said as he sat in the other chair opposite her and pressed a hidden button on the underside of the table.

The glasses sitting on the table rattled a bit for a second before the bottom dropped out. The table, chairs, and a section of floor right next to her shot down several hundred feet deep underground, then stopped as abruptly as it started. When Aleshia's stomach caught up with the rest of her, she sipped her tea and smiled. "That was quite a ride."

"Yes I suppose it is. I do it all the time, so I guess I am use it to it. Come my dear," he said getting up, "I will give you the short tour."

Most of Fenton's true establishment was far underground, hidden from Mechand scanners. Aleshia saw boxes, high end electronic components, all sorts of energy weapons, both hand held and vehicle based. Energy supply systems, refueling systems, even a decent sized clothing store. And she had only seen a small part of the large cavern.

"Wow, you can't just be holding all of this for us?"

"Well," Fenton smiled leaning on a large create with its electronic keylock glowing brightly, "not for you specifically perhaps. But I have always been one to hope for the best, prepare for the worst."

Aleshia looked around again. "I can certainly see that." She felt drawn to the clothing section. Racks of various clothes hung in sealed plastic bags. There were some elegant items, but most of it was more practical."

"Ah, I can see the lady would like a new change of clothes? I have more than what is here in another section, and if you like, I can show you."

"No, no, thank you anyway. I don't have any ration credits to give you. Well I do, but if I used them ... Well–"

Fenton raised a hand. "Say no more, I know exactly what you mean. Hmm, tell you what. I owe Deven anyway, you can take two sets on the house. Deal?"

"Oh no, I couldn't do that. But thank you for the offer."

"Hey it is my gift. Now just go pick out a few things and we will move them upstairs along with these packs." He said patting the box he leaned on. Aleshia moved closer and saw the small label on the side of the crate said "Synth Concentrate".

Aleshia walked between the various clothing racks for a few minutes and finally decided on a two basic outfits in blue and black. They were both pantsuits with a matching top, and jacket. Not fully casual, but not dressy either, somewhere in-between. "I will take these two," she said smiling.

"Okay, but I saw you eyeing that one nice denim set with its included skirt option. Go ahead and grab it." He said with a smile.

"But I wouldn't dream of imposing, you said two, and here are two."

"Hey, you let me decide what is imposing okay?" Fenton grinned as he pushed back a lock of white hair over his ear. "Just go get it. And a lady needs underwear. There is some on the other rack."

"But–"

"No buts. Now go get them before I change my mind." He said with a wink.

A moment later she returned with several packages of

underwear and the denim set. Fenton had already moved the synth packs over near the table and chairs. "Good now take a seat and we will head up. I don't want you falling over," he winked again.

Aleshia sat down and Fenton hit the hidden button. The platform came to life, but this time in reverse. In a moment they were sitting back inside his store as though they never left with the hot afternoon sun glaring through the windows. Aleshia looked at the two synth crates with their status lights blinking green. "I am not sure how I will get those moved into my car. Are you sure they will fit? Or will I need to make two trips?"

"They will fit. No worries. There is an anti-grav system built into these crates. I can move it in there no problem."

"Oh good and thank you. I don't know how to repay you for all you have given me."

"Hey, I told you they are on the house, Deven and I are mates. But if you really want to repay me, then rid the world of the Mechands!"

"We are working on that. Though I don't know exactly how, but I have the feeling Deven has a plan."

Fenton nodded. "You bet he does. I don't know what it is, but I am sure it is a lulu," he said laughing.

Aleshia opened the large storage compartment in the back of her car and Fenton carefully navigated the two large containers into it, then shut down the hover system. "There you are. All ready to go. Oh and here are the emitters also on the order," he said handing over a small box just larger than Aleshia's hand, "and remember about the extra weight. It will take more thrust to speed up or stop with these synth packs."

Aleshia's dark red hair waved as she nodded. "Thank you,

I will keep that in mind." She said moving her seat forward, placing her new clothes in the back seat, then moving the seat back and climbing in. "Thank you again Fenton, for everything."

"You are welcome my dear. And I am sure I will see you again soon." He said with another wink, while backing up so that Aleshia could take off. She engaged the hover systems and gently levitated into the sky.

She keyed in a return to the *Defiant* and engaged the system. But fifteen minutes later the Auto-Nav disengaged flashing indicating something in her path. Her grip on the steering wheel tightened as she activated manual control.

Approaching slowly, she did see something ahead. Then her blood turned cold. A Mechand! Here! Her mind whirled with possibilities and she could only come up with one conclusion: it must have tracked her. She shoved the car into high and started backing away as fast as she could. But the Mechand shot forward and grabbed her front bumper before she could get out of range. She jammed the wheel from one side to another, going in all manner of directions trying to shake it off. But it held fast. She saw a rock formation a little distance away. She headed for it at high speed. Preparing to scrape the Mechand from the bumper, or ram it into the rock.

"Miss Aleshia! Please! I mean you no harm! It is I, Miles!" It shouted trying to overcome the noise of the engine, and swirling air.

Aleshia pushed a button to roll down a window slightly. "Miles?! That is not possible!"

"I assure you it is. Please stop!" he shouted.

"No way!" She dove head long for the rock face.

"Please!"

There was something in his voice. Something Aleshia

never heard before. She jammed on the reverse thrusters and managed to stop just short of crushing the machine that had attached itself to her car. She pinned him to the rock face, and she placed her foot on the accelerator.

"All right. Talk, and quick! I have the car's reinforcement field on. If I hit the peddle, you'll be a crushed tin can. Got it?"

"Thank you. It is I. I tried to talk to you before but you disabled communications. I left the Nexus, I could not, nor will not ever harm you or anyone else. The Nexus tried to take control of my systems. Tried to download my private data on you. I couldn't let that happen so I pulled out the central relay." He said pointing to the large hole in his chest.

"I don't know ..." Aleshia said placing her foot a little more firmly on the peddle.

"Please Miss Aleshia!   I managed to trace our last conversation to this area. My only concern is for you. You were having those bad headaches. I have doomed myself by removing the central relay, it should have terminated my functioning immediately. I chose to terminate myself instead of giving the Nexus data on you. Isn't that enough?"

"How can you feel concern?"

"Miss Aleshia, you forget I am one of the latest models. Although my body is not the latest design, my internal systems are. Actually I am one of the few that have this programming. I have not shown it in fear of it being removed. I found out the Nexus considered it a dangerous error and had any models showing the signs to be wiped. I didn't want to be wiped, so I kept quiet. My feelings tightly hidden, in fear that if found out, I would be destroyed or brain wiped. Which I feel is the same thing."

A tear rolled down her cheek, and she knew Miles was

telling the truth. For here was a Mechand that ripped out a large portion of his middle just to prevent giving data that the Nexus wanted. Risked his own existence, an existence he cherished almost as much as her. "I believe you Miles. I believe you."

Miles bowed, his tarnished dome glinting in the bright sun. "That is good to hear Miss Aleshia. But I must tell you, I do not know how long my backup systems can maintain my continued existence. The relay was never designed to be removed. In fact it had protection circuity to prevent removal. I am surprised that I have made it this far."

"I think I may know someone that might be able to help." She said backing up, then waved him into the car as she popped open the passenger door. He floated in, shut the door, and she hit the overdrive.

A short time later they were landing at the *Defiant*. But as she got out, she found many large energy carbines leveled in her direction. "How *dare* you bring a Mechand here!" Galina sneered preparing to fire on Miles who had just floated out of the car's passenger seat.

"Wait!" Aleshia said as she stood in front of Miles. "Don't! He is okay!"

Galina glared. "He is a Mechand! They in imprison and kill us at every opportunity!"

"And he is not one of them. He is a Mechand yes, but he is not part of the Nexus. I assume you saw that big hole in his chest?"

Galina nodded. "Yes, what of it? It makes a great target."

"It is where his Nexus relay was located. Rather than give away information about me, he pulled it out himself risking his life. His backups managed to maintain his systems, barely. He is no danger to us."

Galina snorted. "Yeah right. Get out of the way Aleshia!"

"No I won't," Aleshia said standing fast.

"What is going on here?" Deven said as he approached.

"Deven! Aleshia brought a Mechand here! Here! Will you talk some sense in to her?"

Deven looked at Aleshia and noticed the hovering Mechand behind her. "Aleshia, what is going on?"

"Deven, this is Miles. He risked his life to keep the Nexus from accessing data he had about me. Then he came here to help. Not to do us harm. The backups that are keeping him going are not going to last much longer. I thought Leon might be able to take a look."

Deven rubbed his chin. "I don't know. I am more inclined to go with Galina on this one."

"Look, just keep a couple of people watching him. If he does anything odd, one shot will probably finish him off. And in the mean time, put the *Defiant* in overdrive. If he is transmitting something, no one will catch us."

Miles floated up and over Aleshia into everyone's clear line of sight. "Mr. Deven, do what you think is best. I will not risk Aleshia or you. If you think it is better to end my existence, then please do so. Just be quick about it. I do not wish to feel my systems shutting down."

"Wait a minute! Since when do Mechands feel?" Deven said leaning forward.

"It is a trick!" Galina shouted stepping in front of Deven.

Miles raised his arms into an upright position. "I assure you it is no trick. I am a programming error. I should not feel but I do. I have kept it hidden all of these years as I did not wish to be reformatted or destroyed. Which is the Nexus' policy." He turned towards Aleshia then back to Galina. "If you feel that it is best to end my existence, then please do so. I do not wish to cause anyone harm." He said hovering over to Galina, placing the barrel of her energy carbine directly into the misshapen hole so prominent in his chest.

Galina started to squeeze the trigger, then stopped. "Bah I can't do it." She said pulling the energy rifle out of Miles' chest. "All right get Leon to give this guy the once over. That is, if you agree, Deven?"

Deven nodded. "Yes I don't see any harm in that. And three people will keep watch on him at any given time. This ship does have a brig with electro cells. Put him in one of those, if he is transmitting or tries to, we will know it instantly."

"Agreed." Galina said as she gave a motion for two other men to surround Miles. "Miles follow us, and anything funny and I will do what I probably should have done in the first place."

Miles inclined his head dome. "I will give you no trouble. And I thank you for believing me."

"I don't know if I believe you, but for *now* I am willing to have Leon check you out." She said with a slight edge in her voice.

Leon was already down in one of the electro cells waiting for Miles when they arrived. "I heard I had a chance to check out an operational Mechand up close and personal." He said with a grin while gesturing towards a makeshift analyzation table. "Deven doesn't want to waste any time."

"Yeah, find out if this thing is transmitting. Oh, he also says he pulled out some sort of Nexus control rather than give away information. You need to give it a real once over."

Miles turned toward Galina. "You can call me Miles. To be honest, I never did like being called an *it*."

Leon raised an eyebrow. "Okay this guy is different. I will give him the once over and let you all know."

Half a day later Deven sat in his cabin with Aleshia, Leon and Galina. "All right what did you find out? You have been babbling stuff for the past several hours."

Leon laughed. "But I haven't left the cells!"

Deven tapped his forehead. "But I heard you. I couldn't help it. I gather you are excited about something."

Leon stood and paced the floor. "You bet I am. I have not seen anything like Miles. He literally has emotions. He feels. I have no idea how, nothing points to any reason for it, yet there it is. And he is right, there was a central control relay built into his chest. It was tied into everything. All evidence points to him pulling it out just as he said."

Aleshia nodded. "I thought so. I told you he isn't here to harm us."

Deven raised his hand. "What else did you find Leon?"

"Well, he is also right in that his backups weren't designed to replace every system he has. Which is about what they are doing. I think they will give out in about two days. Perhaps sooner."

Aleshia sprung to her feet. "Isn't there anything you can do?"

Leon stopped pacing looked out the large window and turned back to face them. "I could jury-rig something to extend that. How long I am not certain. His main systems are not able to function without that central relay. Which I am sure is by design. To be honest, he shouldn't have made it this far."

Deven stood from behind his desk. "Okay, Leon see what you can do for him. Perhaps he could be a help around here."

Galina gasped. "Deven! You can't be serious! He is a Mechand!"

Deven glared at her. "I am serious. And I don't think he is a danger."

She snorted. "And you didn't think bringing in Aleshia was a danger either."

"Tell you what, Leon can install a self-destruct that we can activate should it be necessary. Right Leon?"

Leon rubbed his chin. "Sure I can do that. It is a whole lot easier to rig him to blow up than stay together, given his current condition."

"Okay do it. But I want the control. Agreed?" Everyone nodded. "Good now that is settled, I think we had better finish up on the weapons systems, just in case the Nexus is somehow able to track Miles. If we have an encounter, I want to pick the time. Not the other way around. Leon, how long?"

Leon gazed out the window at the clouds below. "Not sure, could be a day, perhaps two. We are talking very delicate work here."

Aleshia frowned. "I thought you said he only had a day or two left with his backups?"

Leon turned around. "I did."

Aleshia sighed. "Well I'm sure Miles would agree a small chance is better than none. Please do it with care and let me know when you are finished." She said over her shoulder as she walked out of Deven's cabin.

Leon's head lamp shone brightly as he worked inside Miles. He had cobbled together a Mechand repair station using various components from the *Defiant*. He held his breath as he slowly soldered a tiny module into place. It wasn't an exact match, but he hoped it would do the same job as the original, minus the Nexus control. For the past thirty-two hours he had been in here working on this device. Using the various equipment scavenged from the *Defiant* enabled its creation, but the big question was: would it even work?

Oh sure he had the basic outline and design, but that is nothing compared to an operational device. He soldered a few more connections and wiped his brow. It was done. Now to see if it worked.

"Miles can you hear me?"

Miles' dome turned towards Leon who was standing off to the side of the table. "Yes, I can hear you."

"How do you feel?"

"Scared."

Leon's heart sank. "And anything else?"

"I am not certain."

"Try accessing your primary systems."

"But if I do that, and it fails, my backup system will also fail."

"Yes I know. It is the only way."

"All right Mr. Leon, I will try it."

"Would you like me to bring down Aleshia now?"

"No, I would rather she not see this, if it does not work."

Leon nodded. "Okay, give it a try."

There was silence as Miles switched over his systems. Then his chest sparked, then another even bigger one. Leon ran forward and saw one of the contacts wasn't holding. He swore grabbing thick insulated gloves, tools, and quickly tried to secure it. A moment later the sparking stopped. "Miles are you there?" He waited several minutes before asking again. "Miles?" Still no reaction. He swore again as he shut down the field began leaving the electro cell.

But just as he reached the door on the far side of the brig he heard a faint whine. He ran back just in time to see Miles' chest hole glow, blink, then glow again growing brighter. The center module he installed glowed with power and showed its operational status. But had it been in time? He leaned over. "Miles?"

Miles' dome turned one way then back to Leon. "I ... I ... I think, therefore I am."

Leon smiled. "Well many people have been debating that for centuries. But I think you will make it. How are your systems now?"

"Operational. There is a slight sine-wave reverberation in my chest that is odd. But otherwise I seem to be in working order."

"Good. I do hope you realize that this is a patch at best. And I can't say how long it will last." Leon said as he fitted a plate over the hole on Miles chest and secured it.

"Yes I know. And I appreciate all you have done. You have at least given me a chance at continued existence. It is more than anyone else would have done." Miles said as he sat up, extended his legs to the floor and activated his hover systems. A slight glow emanated from his feet as they engaged and he floated up a couple of inches. "Where is Miss Aleshia? I would like to tell her the good news if I may?"

Leon nodded. "Of course. And after that, could you help me reinstall these systems? I had to remove many of them from the *Defiant* to help with your recovery."

Miles inclined his dome. "Certainly Mr. Leon, I would be happy to help in any way possible."

"Good and please just call me 'Leon'. Okay?"

"But my programming requires that I address you properly."

"And you can override that, correct?"

"Yes."

"Then do so. Besides, I think we have reached the first name basis don't you?" Leon said grinning.

Miles inclined his dome further. "Of course, Leon, and I thank you."

"You are welcome. Now go tell Aleshia and get back down here to help me."

"Of course." Miles said as he floated out, stopped then floated back. "Where might she be located?"

"Her quarters is four decks above starboard side."

Miles inclined his dome. "Thank you. I shall return shortly." He said heading off to the decks above.

Several fighters spewed red energy bolts that reflected harmlessly off the *Defiant's* shields.

"How did they find us!?" Deven said as he pointed to the black dots on his screen circling them at high speeds.

"I bet it was that bot that we picked up," Galina said though gritted teeth.

"We have been moving ever since Miles came aboard, correct?"

"Yes we sure have, so how else would they have found us?"

Leon leaned over his console. "I don't know how they found us. But I do know we have a problem. While our shields are operational now, they won't last long. I haven't finished the upgrades and they are quite weak compared to the power that they are blasting us with." He said pointing to the two fighters approaching for another run.

Deven sighed. "Can we outrun them?"

Leon shook his head. "We can outrun even the *Carbonia* carriers, but not a fighter. They are just too fast. I suspect the Mechands are just trying to slow us down until one of their carriers arrive to finish the job."

Another blast hit the shields sending deep vibrations

throughout the *Defiant*. Deven checked one of the consoles. "How are the *Defiant's* weapons? Are they online?"

"Yes, but the targeting systems are not. I had to take them offline when repairing the shields."

"Can they be fired, anyway?"

"Yes but no way to hit anything, you will be firing blind."

"Get two men down there to try it. We can't just sit here. Also keep moving, don't make it easy for them to get a lock on us."

"We are not exactly nimble at the moment," Leon sighed, "but I will see what I can do."

The shields glowed brightly as several more blast hit them straight on. The intercom crackled. "Gregory here. We are in main weapons control. Power is online. How do you want us to proceed?"

"Gregory, just fire in the general direction. I will give you rough coordinates, and fire as quickly as you can." Galina said as she sent coordinates down to the main weapons control room.

"Locations received. Commencing weapons fire." He said as a large bolt shot from one of the energy cannons on the *Defiant's* port side. Then a second later the starboard cannon aft cannon fired. "Only two cannons are responding. Continuing fire." Bolts shot out again and again missing every time by a large margin.

"Try firing on these new path coordinates, also try an elliptical pattern. Mechands usually like to stick to preprogrammed attack vectors." Galina said as she sent down new targeting information.

"Received. Commencing fire." Gregory said over the intercom. A moment later one of the small fighters erupted in a ball of flames.

"You got one!" Deven said into the intercom. "Now see if you can get the other."

"We are trying. But I think this one has changed tactics."

"Yes I am afraid so," Galina groaned, "sending you a new path."

"Received. Trying now." Gregory said as they entered a new attack pattern and bolts of pure red energy lanced out again and again. The Mechand fighter kept dodging them with ease as it raked the *Defiant's* shields with another barrage of energy blasts.

"Shields are going to collapse in less than three minutes." Leon said as his fingers flew over his console. "I have done all I can. Once the shields go down, then we are sitting ducks. I wish I could have finished the repairs."

Miles hovered onto the bridge. "May I be of some assistance?"

Galina glared at the Mechand. "What is *he* doing here?"

"I saw the conflict and wished to offer my assistance."

Aleshia shook her head. "I don't see how you can help the shields are just about gone. After that, the fighter will be able blast us out of the sky."

"And I assume you have weapons at your disposal?"

"Yes but the targeting systems are down." Deven said watching the shield indicators reduce to the verge of total collapse as another blast hit them.

"I may be able to assist that situation. If someone where to show me to the weapons control room. I can act as the targeting system."

"You!?" Galina glared at him. "Over my dead–"

Deven raised his hand. "If he can help, do it. We have little choice."

"All right," Galina grumbled.

"I will show him," Leon said standing, "I am the only person that can hook up his systems anyway."

"Go," Deven said looking at the screen pointing, "I don't think we have more than a couple of minutes."

"I know! I know!" Leon said as he ran out of the room. Miles followed behind him, hovering a few inches off of the deck. Less than a minute later they were in the weapons control room.

"What is he doing here?" Gregory said as he jabbed a finger in Miles' direction while continuing to fire. Hoping one of his shots would be lucky.

"He is here to help." Leon said as he opened a side panel on one of the consoles.

"Please connect my main external sensors to the targeting control systems." Miles said as he opened a panel in his arm, pulled out a glowing data cable, and handed it to Leon.

"Does Deven know about this?" Gregory said standing.

Alarms went off everywhere in the room as the shields collapsed.

"Yes and no time to talk." Leon said as he took the cable and connected it to the fire control console. He then accessed the controls and enabled the data link. "Okay Miles, see what you can do."

Miles' dome nodded forward. "Acknowledged. I have access. Targeting the craft." Miles said as a screen lit up showing the fighter turning for another approach.

"Hurry Miles! We lost our shields. He can do too much damage if he is allowed to fire."

"Understood. Target locked. Activating primary weapons." Miles said as the fighter's weapons glowed preparing to release their deadly onslaught. The *Defiant's* energy cannons opened fire in a precise barrage that the fighter had to abort and make a quick turn to avoid.

"You missed!" Leon breathed.

"Correct. His systems are of a higher level than I expected. I have adapted, it will not happen again." The fighter turned and head back to fire, but before he could get close, one high power energy beam shot out. The fighter dodged it but that brought it into perfect alignment with the port side. Another deadly beam shot out, and the fighter erupted in a ball of fire, shrapnel and burning fuel spraying harmlessly in all directions.

"He did it!" Gregory said wide-eyed. "Well I'll be, he actually did it."

"That is correct, I can assume by your voice patterns you did not expect me to succeed? I do not know why, the armament of this ship is far in excess than that of a fighter, even in its diminished capacity."

"Never mind." Gregory said sitting back down at his console.

"Please disconnect me from the system," Miles said raising his arm, "I wish to verify that Aleshia is unharmed."

Leon turned off the connection and removed the cable from the console. "Okay, there you go. And *nice* shooting."

Miles nodded his dome. "Thank you." He said hovering out of the room and up the stairs.

"Better follow him," Gregory said jerking a thumb towards the door, "I will put that panel back on."

"Thanks." Leon said as he ran out the door. When he finally caught up to Miles, he was already on the bridge.

"Are you all right Miss Aleshia?" Miles asked.

"Yes I am, thanks to you. You saved us."

"I only wanted to assist. I am glad I was able to do so."

Galina stood with her arms folded across her chest. "I still don't trust him. I think it is all a trick of some sort."

Aleshia blinked. "How?"

"I think he brought the Mechands here."

"I say again: How? He doesn't have any transmitters or anything. Leon made sure of that."

"I don't know, but I still think he did it. He is a Mechand, how can we really know what he is programmed for, or what he is capable of."

"He just saved us! What more do you want?"

Deven stood up from the console he was sitting at. "I think Miles has proven himself. I do not see him as a problem unless you can show some other evidence."

Galina snorted. "No, I can't."

"Then I don't want to hear one more word about this. Leon, keep us moving and finish repairing the systems. I don't want a repeat of this until we are ready."

Leon nodded. "Of course," he said then turned towards Miles, "Miles, do you have repair schematics?"

"Unfortunately I do not have any for this particular model of ship. However, I do have them for various systems that are incorporated here. Since the general design is similar, I believe I can be of assistance."

"Excellent, I will show you how to install the new emitters."

Miles inclined his dome. "Of course, I only wish to be of assistance."

As Miles and Leon left, Galina closed the hatch after them. "I still don't think we can trust him."

"Galina, what did I say?" Deven said looking at her in the eye.

"But!"

"Listen of all the people here, you know how I feel about the Mechands. And I am willing to give this one a chance. He has proven himself enough to at least warrant a real chance."

Galina glared at Deven, but knew she was on the losing side of this argument. "I suppose." She sighed rolling her eyes.

"Look if you ever have any proof he can't be trusted, then tell me. Until then, this matter is closed."

Galina's eyes narrowed further then jabbed a finger in Deven's direction. "All right, but mark my words, this is a mistake." She said as she stormed off of the bridge.

Aleshia squeezed Deven's shoulder slightly. "He will be fine. You will see."

"I hope so Aleshia, I hope so." He said placing his hand on hers and looked into her eyes. They shared a moment, a moment where deeply hidden emotions were bubbling to the surface, a moment that scared Aleshia and she was the first to break it.

"Well I need to go unpack my car. In all the excitement, I totally forgot. Can I just take the synth concentrate to the kitchen?"

"Of course." Deven said nodding as he forced his gaze down and picked up the data tab from the console. He was still staring at it when Aleshia left the bridge.

She found her car still on the top deck and brought it into the hold. Popping the trunk she hovered the packs of synth up two decks to the kitchen area. Finding no one there, she maneuvered them next to a set of nearly empty synth packs, set the controls on top, and left.

Aleshia went back to her car, grabbed the items that Fenton gave her, and headed for her cabin. She smiled as she walked looking forward to trying on her new clothes. The one denim outfit was little more dressy than the others, and she probably shouldn't have got it. It certainly wasn't practical in the current situation. But she knew both of the pantsuits would be okay and would look good on her. Arriving at her cabin she placed everything on the bed and closed the door. Picking up one of the packages of underwear she noticed something odd. There were several plain panty sets, but there seemed to be several extra packages as well. Opening them she found seven very nice matching silk bra and panty sets in various colors. And two full teddies. One black and one red. She scratched her head as she looked through everything a second time and noticed a small handwritten note tied to one of the teddies.

"Yes I added a few extra items to your choices. I hope you don't mind. I think you will look lovely in them. And a lady such as yourself should have them. Heck not many ladies come by these days, so I would rather have you enjoy them." The note was signed Fenton Vara.

Then on the back she found something further, in the same handwriting. "P.S. Don't you even think about repaying me. They are yours. And if you need anything else, you just let me know."

12

Leon wiped the sweat from his forehead. All the days excitement had taken their toll, but he had to get these emitters replaced. After, he could sleep. He just finished another when Miles floated in on his anti-grav system.

"Did you replace all of those emitters already?"

"No, I did not."

"Why not?"

"Because I feel I should warn you that we will have–"

Red warning alarms flashed all over the consoles before Miles could finish and an alert came over the intercom. "We have incoming!" Deven's voice came through the speaker. "Leon! Where are you!?"

"What the . . . ?" Leon said as he ran over to click transmit on the intercom.

"I was trying to tell you, I found a beacon attached on the upper deck outside wall." Miles said extending an arm with a small crushed cylinder in his hand. "I suspect it was planted from the last fighter when the shields were down."

"I'm replacing shield emitters. What is going on?" Leon said.

"We have several fighters coming in fast. Larger than the last two. Are the shields back online?"

Leon sighed. "Somewhat."

"What does that mean?"

"I have 3 emitters replaced. So we have some, but not full power."

"I replaced the one unit on the starboard side as you instructed. So you have a total of four," Miles said.

"Great," Galina groaned, "How in the world did they find us so fast?"

"I think I have an answer to that. Miles found a beacon attached on the hull. Looks like the last fighter tagged us after the shields went down. How long until they get here?"

"Less than two minutes," Deven said.

"Okay activate the shields, the power will be balanced since Miles finished his. I will be right there, after I connect Miles into the firing control." Leon said as he clicked off the intercom. "Come on Miles, we need to get to weapons control."

Miles inclined his dome. "Acknowledged." He said floating out of the room following Leon down the maze of bulkheads and corridors. Over a minute had passed by the time they got to the weapons control room.

Gregory smiled as he leaned back his chair and jerked a thumb towards the already removed access panel. "We heard you were coming down. Everything is ready."

"Thanks." Leon said as Miles extended his connection cable, plugged him into the system, and then activated the connection. "Okay try it now." He said as the first blasts raked off of the shields.

"I have control. However, these fighters are far more advanced than the previous ones. Faster, more maneuverable, and with more sophisticated weapons. I count three with several others approaching fast. The odds I will be able to take them all out, is very remote."

"Do what you can Miles. And Gregory, if you can help, do it. I'm heading up to the bridge."

"You got it. Although this bot can shoot better than all of us combined." He said while checking the scanners.

"Activating main weapons." Miles said as a barrage of concentrated energy blast lanced out again and again from the fighters.

Leon ran onto the bridge and sat down at his console checking systems. Deven looked over to him. "How are the shields?"

Leon's fingers flew over the controls. "They are holding for now. But I can't say for how long. While we do have four emitters, that is still half strength, and these fighters are a lot more powerful than the last two."

Several of the *Defiant's* cannons lashed out at the same instant at one target. The fighter was fast and maneuverable but it couldn't avoid all of them at once. It erupted into a exploding fireball when Miles hit the main fuel system.

"Got one!" Galina said as both arms shot up with clenched fists.

"I do not know if that same technique will work again, but I will continue to test more possibilities." Miles' voice came over the intercom.

"Just do what you can Miles." Deven said pointing at one of the screens. "Leon I assume we can't out run these either?"

Leon shook his head. "No, Miles said these are more advanced than the last fighters, and we couldn't outrun those."

"That is correct," Miles said over the intercom, "the previous fighters were a single pilot design, these have three interconnected pilots, larger engines, and more powerful weapons."

The *Defiant* shook as another barrage of energy reflected off of the shields.

"Shields are down to fifty percent. I suspect they will fail in five minutes," Leon sighed.

Several of the *Defiant's* cannons fired at once over and over again along a random trajectory. "Miles what are you doing?" Aleshia said over the intercom.

"Trying something." He said as two of the fighters banked to avoid the *Defiant's* cannons and ended up hitting each other exploding on contact. "And it looks to have been successful."

"Wow. Very impressive Miles," Deven said.

"It would be to our advantage if the same technique would work again. I detect six more ships inbound, they will be here in less than a minute."

The shields flashed as another barrage began. Galina tried to evade them, but the *Defiant* just wasn't built for agility. "Bah! This ship flies like a wheel sunk halfway in the mud. Slow and steady but she just can't out maneuver those fighters."

"Well at least we are not making an easy target." Deven said hanging on to a console.

"No, but some of us might lose their lunches soon," Galina joked.

"Deven, I am not sure about this, but I think I see one of those Mechand *Carbonia* carriers. It is just on the edge of scanners and approaching fast." Aleshia said pointing to the screen front of her.

Deven made his way over holding on to whatever he could as Galina continued to try to avoid the fire fight. "Dang it!

Yes that is one. I can tell by the energy signature. And they always travel in pairs, or at least they always have."

The shields indicators flashed over and over as the power level continued to decline. "Deven, the shields are going to give out in another minute or two. I am trying to reinforce them, but they just aren't ready for this kind of firefight." Leon said as his fingers flew over the keys.

Aleshia looked up at Deven. "Deven, what do we do?"

He sighed. "Abandon ship."

"What?! You can't be serious!" Leon exclaimed. "After all of this you are going to junk her?"

"I won't lose everyone for this." He said gesturing over the room. "We will find another way. We have before, and we will again. Get everyone to the vehicles."

"I am not giving up without a fight!" Leon said. "There must be a way to beat these things."

"We are not giving up my friend, we are living to fight another day. If we stay here, we won't." He said gripping one of the consoles to reach the intercom and pressed the all ship button. "Everyone, this is Deven, abandon ship! We can't win this time. Get to the vehicles and wait until the last possible moment to leave. The destruction of the *Defiant* will cover our escape."

"Are you sure about this?" Leon said checking his console.

Deven sighed. "I told you there is no other way. Get to the vehicles. Aleshia, I will join you in your car in a minute."

Alarms flashed all over the bridge. "Shields are down!" Leon exclaimed as a console near him blew under the strain. Sparks lashed out and stung his arm.

"Okay everyone let's move it! Go go go go!" He shouted as everyone ran for the lower decks. Deven stayed behind keying in a new course, then ran off to join the others.

13

The *Defiant* shuddered with each blast from the fighters. Sparks flew from various consoles and energy conduits before exploding a microsecond later. Deven had to grab on to the bulkheads several times just to stay on his feet. He finally made it to the hanger and several vehicles had already hovered off their pads and were leaving out the aft exit, the large hanger doors had slid open the instant Deven gave the order to abandon ship. He found Aleshia in her car and he jumped into the passenger side.

"Deven! What took you so long? This ship is coming apart!"

"I know, let's not stay here. Hit it!" He said pointing to the opening as several parts of the ceiling broke loose under the strain and fell down around them. Then a re-energizing system fell over, sparking then exploding a second later. If not for a large support beam separating them, a chunk of the debris would have impaled the car's engine. "Hurry!"

"I am! I am!" She said pushing her foot down hard on the accelerator. The car lunged forward and not a moment too soon for a large girder fell, scratching the rear bumper. Three seconds later they were outside and heading off in a different direction. "Wait! What were you doing that took so long?" Aleshia repeated looking back at the *Defiant* careening in space as it was raked again and again with weapons fire.

"I had to make sure that they wouldn't think we escaped. Just don't slow down."

"Why?" But the words were barely out of her mouth when a bright flash as the *Defiant* hit a mountain and exploded.

Deven sighed. "That is why! Hit the overdrive!"

"But it can't be that big of a–" The car was shoved forward with tremendous speed as the shock-wave hit. Aleshia fought for control. Sparks erupted from the center controls as the display went dead. "Oh dang it! Whatever that was just took out most of the systems."

"Electromagnetic pulse. I wanted to make sure that their scanners were blinded."

"Yeah well it did a whole lot more than that! We are going down!" She said fighting the controls. The car continued its decent faster and faster. Mountains rushed up at them as Aleshia dove this way and that trying to avoid a collision. But one reached out and the sluggish controls refused to obey. The tip grabbed a exposed wheel sending them into a spin. She fought again as the spin increased. The g-force shoved them back into the seat as their stomachs wrenched.

"We need to eject." Deven said fighting the urge to empty the contents of his stomach.

"No! I can do this!"

"Aleshia! We need to eject! Now!" He said as the ground rushed up at them.

Aleshia reached for the control but her hand was held back by gravity. Deven saw what she was aiming for, he pounded his fist into the control shattering the plastic safety door activating the button below. The exploding bolts went off and the top section of the car flew away. A microsecond later they were shoved down into their seats as rocket motors in the base of their seats ignited blasting them out of the car. A second later the car hit the ground nose first, crumpling, then exploding into an ever expanding fireball.

Their seats separated with the wind as the rocket motors shut down, the hover systems engaged gently lowering them down on the rocky terrain. Deven sat there for a few moments and allowed his head to clear. He felt his belt, relieved that his data tab was still in its bag. Unhooking the auto-harness he tried to stand, then promptly fell over. He shook his head and tried again. This time he stood and looked around. The icy wind cut through him causing his whole body to shake involuntarily. The ground was covered in a thin layer of snow, with rocks sticking out at regular intervals.

"Aleshia! Where are you?" he shouted. There was no response. He looked around at the unforgiving territory, sighed, and started walking off towards a higher point in the mountainous terrain hoping he might spot Aleshia from there.

Grumbling at the cold, he pressed a button on his wrist activating extra insulation in his shirt and pants. Instantly they expanded giving much needed protection from the cold. "I will have to thank Galina for insisting on the thermal adjusting clothing." He muttered as he stumbled along. Two Mechand fighters zoomed over head, looking for survivors. Deven ducked down behind several large rocks as they approached again. He counted his blessings as they continued on, not spotting him.

A little while later, he found Aleshia's seat. But she was nowhere in sight. There were a few footprints, but not enough to clearly follow. "Well looks like I don't have any other choice." Deven muttered as he sat and reached out with his mind. In the distance he could feel her north of him, very cold, and huddling in a tiny cave. *Wait for me there, I am coming Aleshia.* He tried to project into her mind, but hit several barriers. He sighed then opened his eyes, unsure if she heard him or not.

He stood, shook off of the mental exertion and headed north. Several times fighters zooming overhead caused Deven to hide until they left the area. But he managed to reach the cave without being spotted.

"Deven!" Aleshia ran to him embracing tightly. "I thought you didn't make it."

He squeezed her back. "Now why would you think that? We both ejected didn't we?"

"Yes." Then her face changed, and she punched him into the arm.

"Ow! What was that for?"

"That is for not telling me that the *Defiant* was going to blow and take out my car in the process!"

"I did tell you to hit overdrive didn't I?"

"Oh sure, after it exploded! Why didn't you tell me *that* beforehand?"

"There wasn't time. Look I am sorry, but we couldn't risk them tracking us."

"Yeah I know, but you could have warned me. You could have also told me to pack a parka."

Deven laughed. "I guess Galina never told you."

"Told me what?"

"That the clothes she gave you had temperature assist. Here." Deven said pushing a hidden button in her cuff. Her jacket, pants, and other clothing rippled as they increased in thickness giving instant insulation.

"Ohh that feels so much better. Thank you, and no she didn't tell me about that little feature."

"And I am glad she insisted on it, and here I thought it an expense we could do without." Deven said as another fighter flew past the cave.

"I don't understand why they haven't found us yet. They have scanners," Aleshia said pointing.

"The pulse likely blew out their scanners in the same way it took out your car. I think they are reduced to visual only for the moment."

"But didn't they have a carrier en route?"

Deven nodded. "Yes which means we had better get out of here before they arrive. I am sure those fighters will be fully functional."

Aleshia huddled closer to Deven as he sat on the floor. "And where are we going to go? You just blew up the last thing we had."

"Well not the last thing, and I was not about to lose anyone. Equipment we can replace, people we can't."

"I don't know about that. It sure doesn't seem so easy to replace at the moment," she said looking around. "I don't see a showroom around here for cars. Do you?"

"No, but I am sure we will find you one." He said with a smirk.

A large fighter hovered over to their position. Moved a little distance away and landed. A moment later two other fighters landed on either side of the first. The hatch opened on each, and three battle built Mechands emerged. They were roughly human shaped, but had two energy weapons in each arm unit. Their armor reflected the sunlight as it shown into the valley.

Deven motioned, and they moved out of the cave into a

crevasse just in front of it. The Mechands detected movement and their arms raised up. Energy bolts lashed out from the weapons imbedded in their forearms striking the rock face above. The lead Mechand spoke in a metallic sounding voice "Citizen 4543215391428 give up we have you surrounded, you will come with us or you will be eliminated."

Aleshia looked up into Deven's eyes. "Deven what are we going to do?"

Deven looked back into her green eyes. Those eyes could entrap any man's soul, but it had ensnared him long ago, from the day she entered his dreams. He knew she was his soulmate and even if he where to live another 100 years, he would never find another like her. He kissed her ear and whispered. "They only gave my number, not yours. They only know I am here, not you."

Aleshia blinked. "So?"

"I have to go now." He said preparing to stand up.

Aleshia looked at him with an expression of love, fear, and outright anger all at once. "You can't do that! They will *kill* you!"

"I have no choice. If you get away, there is still a chance." He said his voice full of torment.

"But what? A chance at life without you? I can't do that. I …I …love you." She shook as she said it. For it was true. She wasn't sure until this moment. There was something about him, something that he had touched deep inside her. Something she had never felt before. She felt complete when he was around. Aleshia shook again with the realization that he was her true soulmate. He had been all along, but she never acknowledged it …until now. Even after linking with his sleeping mind. Was it her fear that kept her from seeing the truth? Her head rocked back and forth as her mind whirled.

Deven smiled and kissed her deeply. "And I love you, far beyond words. You have been a part of me for longer than you know. My darling, I must go." He said giving her one long final kiss and stood up. Looking down, he saw her love shining as a beacon aimed right at his heart and fell more in love with her now than ever before. Which he did not think was possible. Another blast hit shaking the ground and more debris fell, causing him to duck down again. He pulled her closer and kissed her soft welcoming lips. Fire went between them as the passion burned brighter than a supernova. He felt her knees grow weak and falter.

"I love you, never forget me." He leaped out of the cleft and ran shouting "Right here you metal morons!" They turned and followed him in swift succession.

"No don't!" She reached for him, but was still reeling from the moment they shared and he was already well beyond her reach. Aleshia watched helplessly as he ran. Wondering if she would ever see him again.

— 14 —

Aleshia remained huddled in the cleft, hidden from view of the Mechands. Her eyes filled with tears as they shot again and again in Deven's direction. He ran in unusual patterns, ducking and diving the various energy blasts. He had almost made it to the shelter of a large rock when a crossfire of energy beams intersected catching him in the middle. He froze there for a second as the energy raked over him, and then uncontrollably fell forward. Aleshia held her hand tightly over her mouth, lest she make any sounds to let them know of her position.

Two Mechands approached carefully, and when Deven didn't move they attached a box to his belt and he was encased in a bluish field. His body floated up on an anti-grav cushion and levitated inside one of the fighters. The Mechands then lined up and marched into their fighters. A moment later the gangway closed, and they took off heading south, no doubt to rendezvous with a carrier.

Tears ran down Aleshia's cheeks. Her mind whirled at what to do. She was alone. She stood up from the indentation she was hiding in and prepared to leave when a glint from inside the cave caught her eye. She walked over to it and found the sun had moved just enough to reflect off of the buckle to Deven's belt pack. Picking it up she found his data tab inside. As her finger found the power button, it scanned her fingerprint. Another button blinked in quick succession and she knew it wasn't for low power. Looking closer it was a message waiting light. She pressed the button and a projection of Deven appeared before her.

"Hello Aleshia, if you are seeing this then I am likely dead or worse. I set up my data tab to offer to display this message when it detected your fingerprints. There is so much I wanted to tell you. So much I wanted to do with you. As I told you before, I have known about you for a long long time. I felt you, saw you in my dreams long before we ever met. It was as if our hearts were calling out to each other. I doubt you will believe me, and perhaps it is not true on your end. But it certainly is on mine."

Deven's hologram turned away, then back. "I am sorry I got you into this mess. And it bothers me even more that I contacted you in such a fashion. I struggled with this for weeks. But I knew your time was limited. Soon the Mechands would find out about you, and then I would lose you forever. I couldn't take that chance. It broke my heart to see you run away, and then when we did finally meet properly in Iceland, I feared my heart would burst not being able to embrace my feelings for you.

"But I knew if I did, you would push me further away. I only hope that by the time you see this, you know how I truly feel about you. You are my soulmate, my other half. I can't deny that, but if you don't feel that way, well …" The Deven's face became flushed with anguish, but he fought it off. "The data tab you hold has key information that the Resistance needs. You need to get it to Leon. But whatever you do, it can't fall into Mechand hands. Also I have programed the data tab with the ability to activate a beacon on an encrypted link that only Galina and Leon can access. Once activated, they should be able to home in on your position."

Deven sighed and gestured with his hand in a pointing movement as he spoke. "Be careful though it is possible; however, unlikely that the Mechands could detect the base signal and determine your location. They won't know who it is, but if you are in an area with a lot of transmissions, they will just ignore it. Though in an area with few transmissions it will stand out like a high intensity beam of light in a dark room.

"If you can get the information to Leon, then we can finally destroy the Mechands once and for all. But he can't do it without your help. Your abilities will continue to grow, and in a short while you will be able to destroy them. I just wished I could have been there to see it.

"I can only hope that you can forgive me for placing this burden upon you. It was never my intention. And I am sorry." An alarm went off in the distance and Deven turned away then back again. "I have to go now. Just remember I love you, and always will." He said as the image winked out.

Aleshia wiped a tear before it could fall off of her cheek. She strapped his pack on and headed off in the direction of a town she remembered seeing when they were on the *Defiant*. By the time she reached it, night had fallen. She was about to go in through the main road, when she saw several Mechands on either side of the entrance, she looked around for another way.

An hour later she found a way through the fence and made her way inside. She couldn't see anyone nearby, but on the other side she heard a horse. She moved carefully along the wall and sneaked inside the building to find several horses in various stalls. "The owner must be very rich," she thought, "no one has horses otherwise. They cost too many ration credits." Thankfully the building was a great deal warmer than outside and she curled up a corner and fell asleep.

Sunlight shone in a window striking Aleshia's face, waking her with a jolt. For a moment she forgot where she was, then all the events of the past day flooded back. With a sigh she sat up and tried to stretch the kinks out. Her eyes widened as the barn door swung open with a loud bang. Peeking over the wall she saw a young girl who had kicked open the door, bringing in two buckets of synth oats for the horses. She was tall, but Aleshia could tell she was in her mid teens by the loud fashion of her clothes. Her long blonde hair flowed gracefully over her shoulders as she walked. Aleshia tried to get down quietly but at the last moment her foot slipped and she landed with a thud.

"Who is there?" the girl called out.

Aleshia rubbed her sore hip but remained silent.

"Who is there? I will call my Mechand if you don't show yourself."

Aleshia poked her head around the corner. "I don't mean you any harm. It was cold last night, and I found my way here. I hope you don't mind."

"How did you get here? I haven't seen you around before."

"My car malfunctioned, and I had to eject. The beacon system was damaged, so no one could find me. I had to find shelter, I am sorry if I intruded."

The young woman smiled. "No, that is okay. You were in trouble. My name is Erina. What is yours?"

"Aleshia."

"Nice to meet you Aleshia. Now why don't you come over

to the house? My parents are away today, but I am sure they wouldn't mind helping someone that just had a car accident."

Aleshia shook her head. "Thanks, but I would rather just stay here."

"Why?"

Aleshia looked off then back again. "Well, you mentioned a Mechand."

Erina shrugged. "So? Everyone has one."

"Yes, well, I think it is why my car malfunctioned, so I am trying to avoid them."

Erina cocked her eyebrow. "Must be pretty hard avoiding them. They are everywhere."

"Yes, I know. I didn't realize it till now," Aleshia smiled. "I am glad you came to feed your horses, instead of your Mechand."

"I like to feed them myself." Erina said patting one of her horses as she filled the trough in front of him with fresh synth. "And I think they eat better if I do it."

"Perhaps they don't like Mechands either," Aleshia joked.

Erina chuckled as she filled the other troughs. "You may be right."

"Would you mind if I stay here for a little while?"

Erina shrugged. "Not at all. Do you need anything?"

"Well I am a bit hungry. But I don't want to intrude."

"Oh don't worry about that. I will get you a synth bar. Anything else and my Mechand will want to ask me why, or perhaps follow me. I think my parents programmed it to be a little more watchful than they needed," she said with a wink.

"That would be great, thank you."

"You are welcome. I will be back in a blink."

Aleshia stayed out of sight, and a few minutes later Erina returned. She tossed Aleshia a wrapped bar, and an apple flavored drink box. "There you go. It was all I could bring without arousing suspicion. I hope you like chocolate, it is the flavor I got on the bar. It is the only type I like, my Mechand would get worried about me otherwise."

"I like chocolate, thank you."

"You're welcome. If you change your mind about coming up to the house, you're welcome to anytime." Erina said as she opened the door.

"I will keep that in mind. Thank you again."

"Welcome. See ya!" She said as the door closed behind her.

Aleshia unwrapped the bar, took a bite, and frowned. Raw synth bars always tasted the same, no matter the flavor. But at least the drink washed the taste from her mouth. She sighed, ate the rest of it quickly, and washed it down with the rest of the drink box. She tossed the bio degradable wrapper and box into a waste bin which quickly vaporized them, and leaned back against the wall of the empty stall.

She pulled out Deven's data tab and looked over the various files. Nothing stood out as a way to destroy the Mechands, so what could he have meant? She did find a way to activate its transmission beam scanner. The results were not good. There were a few, but not enough to hide in a sea of other noise. But when she checked the clock, the reason was obvious. Most people were just waking up, and peak traffic wouldn't be for some time. Aleshia powered off the data tab and settled in for a long wait.

She awoke sometime later. Checking the data tab proved fruitful, several hours had passed and there was just enough traffic to make an attempt. She was about to activate the link when she heard a loud conversation outside.

"Metlo, where are you going?" Erina called.

The large Mechand stopped its forward movement, turned

its roughly human head around. "Miss Erina, you know that I always clean the stable today at this time. It is the only thing you allow me to do in the stables. I am surprised at your question."

"Well I was just down there, and it doesn't need cleaning today."

"That would be highly unusual. I haven't cleaned it for two days."

"Yes well I am certain it can skip today."

"Is there a problem with the stables?"

"No not at all, why do you ask?"

"Your motions and voice patterns indicate otherwise." The Mechand said as he turned his head around and continued walking towards the stables.

"Oh dang it," Aleshia muttered, "I can't let him see me." She gazed around the stables but couldn't find any place to hide. Then looked up and smiled.

Metlo burst through the stable doors. He craned his neck joint from one side to the other. Walked towards the back, and checked every stall.

Erina ran into the stables, quickly looked around. But Aleshia was nowhere to be found. "See I told you, nothing here."

"Yes, it would seem that I am in error. However, the stalls do need a cleaning."

Erina looked up and her eyes went wide for a second upon seeing Aleshia in the rafters above them. She quickly looked back at Metlo. "Yes you are right about that. But would you mind fixing me lunch now? You can do the stalls later."

"It is not your usual time, but if you wish." Metlo said as he inclined his metal head.

"I do. And thank you."

"You are welcome Miss Erina." Metlo said as he walked out of the stables.

Erina looked up at Aleshia and mouthed "Sorry." And ran after Metlo.

Aleshia carefully climbed down to ground level and pulled out Deven's data tab. She activated the scanner and there was still enough traffic in the area to chance a call. She activated the encrypted link and tried to contact Galina.

The connection failed, and after several tries she was about to give up when there was a blast of static. The system indicated that normal power levels were not sufficient and was requesting to boost the signal. But she knew such an increase would drain the power cell quickly. She sighed and engaged the signal boost. Immediately Galina's face resolved on the screen.

"Aleshia! Are you all right? Where are you? Where is Deven?"

"Galina, I don't have much time. I am in some little town not far from where the *Defiant* went down. Can you trace this signal? I don't think I have the power to transmit for long."

"Don't need to, not many towns in that area. We will find you. Where is Deven?"

"I ... I'm not sure."

"What do you mean you are not sure? He left with you, and you are using his data tab."

"He was captured. The Mechands didn't know I was with him. He ran off so they wouldn't find me. I don't know where they took him."

"We will find him, don't worry."

"Oh one thing I will be a mile to the west of the town. There are quite a few Mechands here. I think the guards at the entrance are looking for us." Aleshia said just as the screen showed critical low power error and the transmission cut to save energy. She shut off the data tab to conserve what power was left, put it in the belt pack and peeked outside. No one was around. She quietly left by the back entrance and made her way to the gap in the fencing she found last night. Several times she had to duck around a corner to prevent from being spotted. After what seemed like hours, she found the break. Thankfully it had not been repaired and she slipped out and headed west.

The journey while difficult, was far easier than it was last night. At least now she could see where to put her feet. A few times Aleshia thought she heard a vehicle, causing her to hide among the rocks or under low-lying trees. But nothing ever appeared. After reaching a mile, she hid among a thick patch of trees. The wind blew, and she wished she was back home, or even in those stables. She shivered and checked the data tab and silently cursed. It had been several hours since she talked with Galina, and was starting to get dark. Realization hit her like a bolt of lightning: Galina may not have received all of her message.

Then she heard a faint wine of a distant engine. She huddled down a bit more and peeked out from the trees. A decent sized truck with high intensity lights, hovered overhead then landed softly a short distance away. She squinted in the darkness when a man emerged from the drivers side. Aleshia didn't recognize him in the glare of the lights, and the truck could belong to anyone. She thought about trying to run for it, but she would be seen. And this may be a trap. Another shiver ran through her as an icy wind whipped through the valley.

The man seemed to speak to someone inside, and the passenger door opened. Aleshia could tell this was a woman by her outline in the glare of the lights. "Aleshia! Where are you?" the woman shouted.

"Galina!" Aleshia stood up and waved. "Over here." She shouted running over to the truck.

Galina pointed to the man on the other side. "This is Otis, not sure if you saw him back on the *Defiant*. And why were you hiding?"

"Sorry I had to be sure it was you. With those lights, and losing Deven ..."

Galina raised her hand. "I understand. Get in, if we stay much longer, we are going to draw attention."

"Oh of course." She said hopping into the truck's cab through the drivers door. Otis followed her, and Galina slipped back in through the passenger side.

Otis activated the hover systems, and they rose up, heading off to the nearest skyway. "Glad we found you," Otis said as he engaged the overdrive, "the Mechands are all over the area."

Aleshia nodded her head. "I know. I was lucky to find a stable without Mechands last night."

Galina's eyebrows rose. "A stable without a Mechand? That is unusual. Heck having a stable is unusual in and of itself."

"I know. How many people made it off of the *Defiant*?"

"Pretty much everyone. The only ones missing seems to be Leon and Miles."

"Leon? Oh no."

Galina sighed. "Yes, no one has seen or heard from him since the ship went down."

"What do we do now?"

"Well first we need to free Deven. Do you know where he was taken?"

Aleshia shook her head. "No I don't."

"We were hoping you had an idea. What did Deven say before he was captured?"

"Not much that can help us. He did leave me a message though on his data tab."

"Which was?" Otis asked.

"He talked about a way to destroy the Mechands, but didn't give me any details. He said it is vital that I get the data tab to Leon as it held the key. But I have searched it several times. I don't find anything that shows how to destroy the Mechands."

"That doesn't make sense." Galina said looking out into the dark night.

"I know, but there must be something there, or he wouldn't have told me to get it to him."

"Umm ladies I hate to barge in," Otis said pointing to the nav screen, "but I think we just received a new set of coordinates."

Aleshia blinked. "From whom?"

Otis shrugged. "I have no idea. But it seems to have been sent by someone in Resistance, it has our verification key."

"Couldn't that have been faked?" Aleshia asked.

Otis shook his head. "No way, Leon made sure that only a few of us had the sending key. Heck, I never saw it, let alone had it. I think only Deven, Leon, and Galina here had a copy."

Galina nodded. "Yes that's right. We didn't want to take a chance that someone might get access to it, and be able to send everyone a set of coordinates leading them into an ambush."

"Right," Otis said nodding, "the problem is, do we trust this? If only the three of you had the encryption key, and two are missing. Does that mean the Mechands have the key?"

"Very possible. No way to know though," Galina said as she checked her data tab, "those coordinates seem to be someplace high above old Siberia."

"Siberia? Are you sure? No one goes there since that nuclear accident long ago. Land and you end up a living glow worm." Otis said gripping the control wheel.

Galina tapped several buttons on her data pad. "Yes I am sure, I checked them three times. The coordinates are high above though. Might be safe that high in the atmosphere."

"The question is, do we go? Should we check with everyone else first?" Aleshia said sitting back in the seat.

"We could, but that will take time. This kind of encrypted rendezvous is only good for six hours. After that, we would always move on, just in case it was somehow intercepted."

"Let's go take a look," Otis said engaging the nav system. "we can scan a long distance from whatever it is. If it looks bad, we get the heck out of dodge."

Aleshia shrugged. "It is worth a try."

"All right," Galina said checking her data tab again. "but the first sign of anything odd, and we overdrive out of there."

Two hours later they approached the location. Otis disengaged overdrive and put the scanners on full. "I am not seeing anything unusual, wait, there is something a little distance from us. It is not exactly at the coordinates, but a little west."

"Yes I see it." Galina said trying to adjust the scanners. "Nothing else in range though. If it was a Mechand trap, they would be deploying fighters by now. Head in, but keep your finger on the overdrive."

Otis laughed. "Don't I always?"

As they approached, the image looked more and more like a ship, a carrier but a bit different.

"It's the *Defiant*!" Aleshia exclaimed pointing to the large shape in the distance.

"It can't be!" Galina checked the scanners. "It is not sending out the *Defiant's* encrypted ID Leon installed, so it could still be a trick."

"Or the ID transmitter was damaged during the fight." Otis said with his finger on the overdrive button. "What do you want to do?"

"Let's get out of here." Galina said with a wave of her hand. "I don't like it. This feels too weird."

"Okay will do." He said starting to press the button. But he never finished. The communication screen flipped up, and an image began to resolve. Blocks of encrypted data filed in, and unscrambled themselves to reveal Leon's smiling face.

"Leon!" Aleshia exclaimed.

"In the flesh," he said smiling, "come on in. You are cleared, I have the landing bay open."

"How in the world–" Galina said but Leon cut her off.

"I'll explain when you are aboard. In short the reports of my death have been greatly exaggerated." His smile broadened as the image winked out.

Otis guided the truck in. The front hanger bay was open as Leon said. The *Defiant* was blast scarred but still in amazingly good shape considering what they had seen. "This ought to be interesting." He said under his breath as he landed in an empty area and the doors behind them closed. Pressure seals engaged and the indicator in the far wall flicked from red to green. "And it looks safe to get out."

Galina consulted her data tab, and the trucks scanners. "Yes seems to be. We are high enough up that no one could breathe without pressure and oxygen. Not even Mechand fighters can go up this high without problems. Not many vehicles these days can, we are lucky that most of ours were modified."

"I take it the *Defiant* is back from a time when they could?" Aleshia said looking around.

Galina nodded. "Yes. However, we never tested it. Never saw the need," she shrugged.

"Well I see a need now," Otis said smiling. "Shall we go see the trickster?"

Galina laughed. "Indeed, let's go see what Leon has up his sleeve, besides the *Defiant*."

15

"But we saw the *Defiant* destroyed!" Aleshia exclaimed.

"Ah, you thought you did," Leon grinned, "just what I wanted everyone to think."

"But how?" Galina chimed in.

"It was simple really. The ship was going down, the Mechands thought we had lost all control. I just let them think that. When we were just about to hit the top of the mountain, I managed to phase the ship through it. To cover that up, I ejected part of the old unused power core out the back and detonated it. The explosion blinded their sensors until we were on the other side and far away."

"Remind me to never play poker with you," Aleshia grinned.

Leon laughed. "Oh, I don't know, that could be fun."

Galina swatted him across the top of the head playfully. "You and your dirty mind."

Leon looked at her. "What? I didn't say–"

Galina laughed. "Never mind. But what I don't understand is how you managed to do all of that in the short period of time we had to leave."

"Oh, I couldn't have done it alone. I had help." Leon said, and as if on cue Miles floated into the room.

"Miles!" Aleshia ran over to hug him. "I thought you were destroyed or lost."

"Miss Aleshia, it is good to see you. No I wasn't lost. I have been helping Leon with repairs."

"And saving the ship," Leon said pointing, "don't forget that part."

"I didn't do that much," Miles said.

"Didn't do much? Without him, I never would have been able to eject that old power core in time. He ripped the core right out of the power room and chucked it out the back hanger bay. But not before rigging it to explode three seconds later."

"It was nothing really. I only live to serve," Miles said inclining his dome.

"Yeah yeah, so you keep saying," Leon said.

"What you didn't tell us is how were you able to phase through the mountain with blown out shields?" Galina said with her arms folded.

"Well I never said they were blown out, just useless for deflecting what the fighters were pouring on. But as everyone was leaving I realized that there just might be enough left in them to phase the *Defiant* for a few seconds. And thankfully I was right. But I couldn't risk everyone on that, so I let you leave just in case this didn't work. Miles volunteered to stay on and help."

"Well one last question." Aleshia said grabbing a chair from one of the bridge consoles, sitting down, and looking straight at Miles. "I thought you were in firing control? How did you do that, and eject a power core out the back?"

Miles inclined his dome in Aleshia's direction. "It was a simple procedure. I programmed the weapons to continue to fire in an unusual pattern that gave the illusion that I was still controlling them. At that point there was little chance of me hitting the fighters, but we had to maintain the impression we were trying. That gave enough time to remove the power core and eject it." Miles said hovering over by Aleshia. "I am sorry to have deceived you, but the deception was necessary. Leon was not certain if his plan to phase the *Defiant* would work. And I knew you had already left with Mr. Deven and were safe."

"Okay," Galina said sitting down, "what is the plan now?"

"Beyond getting everyone back aboard. I have no idea," Leon shrugged.

"I do actually." Aleshia handed Leon Deven's data tab. "Deven said he left a way to destroy the Mechands in there. But I don't see any files or data regarding it."

"Hmm," Leon said as he cabled the data tab into his console. "I don't see anything about destroying the Mechands per se. But ... ohhhh my! That little devil!"

"What? What did you find?"

"Deven encoded this so that unless it was cabled into a console with my key, it wouldn't reveal a file. It just did and activated."

"It did what?" Galina shot forward to get a closer look at the data tab.

"As far as I can tell it is just a locator program. And is showing a location in southern Florida."

"Florida? What is there?" Aleshia asked.

"I have no idea." Leon said as he tried to access data on its location.

"Don't bother. I know what it is."

Everyone turned to Otis who just stood there with the largest grin on his face. "Well don't just keep us in suspense." Aleshia said pointing to the screen. "What is it?"

"It is a holding location that Mechands take prisoners. They say it is a processing plant for synth, but others know better."

"And how do you know?" Galina asked.

"A buddy of mine was taken there once. I almost got him out, but the Mechs shot him just as we reached the car. I managed to get away, but it wasn't easy. And that was years ago, I am sure they upgraded the security since then."

"The question is how and why is this directing us there?"

Leon sat back. "I think it is quite obvious, this is Deven. He thought he might be captured and did this as a safety net."

"Some safety net," Galina snorted, "and are you sure it is him and not the Mechands?"

"Yes I am sure. The beacon is with his encoded key, and it needs his DNA to encode properly. I don't see how the Mechands could fake that." As if on cue the beacon disappeared.

"Oh no! Does that mean they found the beacon?"

Leon shook his head. "If I know Deven, this thing only transmits on occasion. A constant beacon could be easily found. But an intermittent one, that is a lot harder."

"Harder for us too," Galina sneered.

"Perhaps, but I can get you there," Otis said. "I know exactly where it is, but beyond that ... " he trailed off.

"If I may make a suggestion." Miles said raising his arm "I know the Mechands more than you do, as I am one, and I think I can help in this situation. Mr. Otis said that they likely upgraded security after trying to help his friend escape. While I agree with this assessment, I also think that since the instillation is trying to maintain its covert nature, the upgrades will be still not be enough to defend against a full out assault. They would be expecting a few simple vehicles, or a sneak attack. But not the full power of the *Defiant*."

Leon's eyes widened. "Why that is brilliant! Of course they wouldn't be expecting that. We can probably blast our way in and get Deven out of there before any reinforcements could be sent."

Miles inclined his dome. "I agree. However, the timing will be critical. Too long and I am sure several *Carbonia* cruisers will intercept us there."

"And I want shields up to full. I don't want to fly in there without them. Or we will be making a repeat of last time," Leon sighed.

"I would be happy to help you with that." Miles said as he hovered over to Leon.

"Good, thanks Miles. Let's get started, we still have a few more people to pick up before we can move anyway."

Several hours later, every shield emitter had been replaced, properly calibrated and powered up to full. Three more vehicles arrived bringing more supplies and equipment thought lost during the evacuation.

Aleshia sat in Deven's chair on the bridge as Leon came in, with Miles floating behind him. "Are we good to go?"

Leon nodded. "You bet. Let's go bust Deven out!"

Aleshia nodded. "Let's go. Galina, engage overdrive. And use that skyway we looked up earlier. The real busy one. It should mask our approach for as long as possible."

"Agreed." She said feeding the coordinates into the Auto-Nav.

Aleshia hit the intercom. "Everyone this is Aleshia, we are about to jump into overdrive, make sure everything is secured. Okay Galina, do it!"

Galina nodded and pressed a button on her console. A second later the *Defiant's* powerful main engines glowed to life, and the ship leapt into overdrive.

16

The *Defiant* swept through the skyway like an energy knife through butter.

Galina chuckled. "I don't think anyone has seen anything as large as the *Defiant* before. They're just getting out of our way."

Aleshia grinned. "Well that is to our advantage. How long until we arrive?"

Galina checked her console. "Hmm I would say we should stay in the skyway for another five minutes. Then we can drop out. Three minutes after that we will be right over top of that installation if Otis is right.

"Hey, I am right. When have I ever led you astray?"

Galina chuckled. "Only kidding Otis, I know you have it right."

Aleshia got to her feet. "Otis can you take me down? I want to be there."

"Are you sure? I think you should–"

"No! I failed Deven once, I am not about to do it again."

"Okay. I have a truck in one of the bays that has been modified with armor and even a small energy canon."

Miles floated over. "Miss Aleshia, I would like to accompany you as well."

"No Miles, Leon might need you here."

Miles lowered his dome and voice. "Very well Miss Aleshia."

Aleshia grabbed Deven's data tab and slipped it into its hip pack, then keyed the intercom. "Okay everyone let's do this," she pointed towards the door, "Otis let's go."

"You got it." He said as they left the Bridge.

A few minutes later Aleshia and Otis were strapped in the armored truck. Grey and roughly rectangular with small images of Mechands sporting crushed heads on the hood, doors, and trunk area. "Don't you think that is pushing it?" She said indicating the small decals.

"Nah, they couldn't see them, and even if they could, they wouldn't get the reference."

"I take it you modified this truck?"

Otis grinned. "Does it show that much?"

Aleshia rolled her eyes. "Just a bit."

The large intercom in the hanger crackled to life. "Everyone, heads up, we are dropping out of overdrive in 5 …4 …3 …2 …1". Everyone felt the lurch as the overdrive disengaged. "Okay, we are less than a minute to target, everyone get ready," Leon's voice boomed.

"Well this should be fun." Otis said grinning as he gripped the control wheel.

"I just hope we all make it back." Aleshia looked out the window as the large hanger doors ground open.

"We will, you'll see." Otis said as he prepared to engage full thrust.

The large intercom crackled again with Leon's voice. "Over target in 3 …2 …1 *EVERYONE LAUNCH!*"

Otis pushed the accelerator down hard and they were shoved back into their seats. A second later they were clear of the hanger. Several other modified cars also exited just before the blue aura of the *Defiant's* powerful shields snapped into being.

Energy blasts exploded all around them as the compound reacted. Thankfully they were a minute too slow. The attack took them by complete surprise. The Mechands managed to launch two fighters before the *Defiant* took out the launch bay.

"I am sorry, they managed to launch two fighters. We will try to get them, but be on the lookout." Leon's voice came over the encrypted link.

"I think they will pose no threat, their systems are outdated compared to mine." Miles said as one of the fighters exploded.

"Okay, we are heading in. Miles cover us."

"Of course," Miles said over the link.

Otis guided the truck with pure precision as he dogged energy blasts and the fighter that had suddenly taken an interest in them. "Dang it! I can't shake him!" Otis said.

"Target acquisition in 5 ... 4 ... 3"

"Miles! Hurry up!" Otis said as another blast shook the truck. "He is too close!"

"2 ... 1 ... target locked." All the *Defiant's* main cannons lashed out at once in a single cohesive force. The fighter missed several blasts but then it was caught in a crossfire and exploded into a fireball of fuel and scrap metal.

"Whew! Thanks Miles."

"Good shooting Miles!" Aleshia said.

"We will be inside in ten seconds." Otis said as he gunned the accelerator.

The ground rushed up at them and Aleshia's eyes went wide. "Otis! Too fast!"

"Hang on!" Otis said as in the last second he pulled up hard on the control and hit the vertical thrust at full burn. Half a second later they were on the ground.

Aleshia blinked and tried to swallow her heart that had made its way up into her throat. "What . . . we are alive? How did you–"

"Do that? It is an old trick I learned, but a buddy of mine died trying it so yes it is risky. However, the Mechands will think we crashed. If we did a normal landing, they would already be here."

Aleshia looked around. "Where are we?"

"The back maintenance area. They don't usually have this part guarded, or used to anyway. We are just inside the main perimeter, the cell areas are to the north."

"Okay," Aleshia said toggling the link, "we are heading in. Keep them busy."

Leon laughed. "That won't be a problem. They are certainly keeping *us* busy." Leon said as another blast impacted the *Defiant's* shields.

"Any problems?"

"No, it is as Otis suspected, they were counting on stealth rather than raw fire power. We can hold our own for now. If a few carriers show up that will change."

Aleshia terminated the link and jerked a thumb towards the entrance Otis had indicated earlier. "Let's go."

"Sure but take this," Otis said tossing her a small energy carbine pistol, "we don't know what we will run into."

Aleshia sighed. "All right, but I warn you, I never shot one of these before."

They got out and ran for the roughly hexagonal shaped door. The area was full of broken hardware of all kinds: Cannons, a fighter, and several Mechands that had obviously seen better days. All the parts had rusted from the exposure to the elements.

"None of this have been touched in a long time," Aleshia said pointing.

"I told you they didn't use it much even back when I was here." Otis said as they reached the door.

"How do we get in? Knock?"

Otis laughed. "No, I have a better method." He said producing a card from his hip pouch that was wired to a tiny keyboard. He inserted the card and hit a few keys. The display on the card quickly began displaying numbers and letters in a blur of motion. Less than twenty seconds later the door ground open. "There we go. They did upgrade the security though, last time it only took me five seconds."

Aleshia rolled her eyes. He was obviously a cracker and lived to break into systems. They carefully moved forward along the corridor. "Where are the cells?" she whispered.

"We should take a right at the end of this corridor, then a left," Otis said pointing.

So far they hadn't seen any Mechands. For an interrogation facility, it seemed remarkably weak in security. They moved past several doors. Aleshia peeked inside one and saw a room full of equipment covered in dust. The next one looked the same. Something was wrong. Very wrong. They heard the distant blasts being exchanged from the *Defiant*, and the facility's cannons, but nothing else. It was almost as quiet as a tomb.

"Otis, this is wrong. It is too quiet."

Otis nodded. "Yeah, I know. It was never this easy." They took a right, and this corridor was just as empty as the last. The rooms along it were either empty or disused and covered in dust. "I don't like this. I think we should get the heck out of dodge."

"Not without Deven."

"If he is here."

"He is, I can feel him." Aleshia said as the continued on. They took a left and arrived at the energy cells. The cells lined the both walls and were recessed areas in white with a bed, although many of them seemed to contain torture devices. All of them were shut down except one on the far end. There behind an energy curtain, lay Deven strapped to some sort of device. His arms were outstretched as were his legs. An odd roughly spherical device stuck out in various directions with cables that ran into the ceiling held his head. He looked very haggard and worn. The Mechands had tortured his mind.

Aleshia and Otis ran to the cell. The field hummed with energy blocking their path. "Deven! Deven! Is me! Are you okay?" Aleshia whispered. She could hear his quiet breaths, but he never stirred. "Otis, can you get us inside?"

"Of course, give me a minute." He said pulling a panel off of the wall and hooked in his little card and keyboard.

"Deven! We will have you out of there in a minute."

Deven's head wobbled a bit and turned inside the device. His eyes slowly focused. "Aleshia?"

"Yes, we came to rescue you."

"It is a trap. Get out of here."

"There got it!" Otis said as the energy field dropped. But a second later several alarms went off and red lights embedded into the walls flashed repeatedly. "Oh dang it!"

Several battle grade Mechands marched into the room. "You have entered this facility without authorization. Surrender or be terminated!" They said in the standard battle tone and raised their arms, containing several energy weapons embedded.

Otis grabbed Aleshia and dove into Deven's cell just as the Mechands opened fire blasting the wall where they were a moment ago. Otis peeked around the corner and fired his carbine. The blast hit one of them dead center of its armor, causing no damage. "I think we're in trouble!" He said as they responded filling the hall with energy blasts. The walls sizzled with the onslaught. They were protected inside the cell, but only until the Mechands advanced. Then they would be in a direct line of fire.

Aleshia pulled the device off of Deven's head, unlocked the straps and helped him from the platform. "I wanted you safe, I didn't want you to come," he said trying to stand, "they used my tracer against me. I was the bait to get you all here."

"Shhhh," she said placing a finger on his lips, "how could I not come and get you. Trap or no trap?"

"I hate to break up this touching reunion, but we have a little problem here." Otis said as he fired off several well placed shots that merely bounced off the Mechand's armor.

Removed from the devices, Deven felt his strength returning and took a peek around the corner. He ducked back just before an energy beam hit. "Try hitting their center optical sensors on the head. It might be the least armored spot."

Otis blinked. "Might?"

"Well this is your rescue. You got a better idea?"

"Heck no. I didn't intend on getting into a firefight with an advanced armored division! Let's try it." Otis said as he peeked around the corner and squeezed his trigger. The energy beam shot one of the Mechands on the center optic sensor, but bounced off. Otis ducked back. "Okay any other ideas?"

"Perhaps if two people shot in the same spot at the same time?" Aleshia offered.

"Okay let's try it. But can you shoot that accurately?"

"No, I told you, I never fired one of these before." Aleshia said holding the weapon in her hand.

"I can. I used to be pretty good," Deven said.

"Pretty good ain't going to cut it here Boss."

"Well I am willing to try."

"Okay let's do it. Aleshia give him the carbine."

Deven took the weapon, peeked around the corner, and frowned. They were still approaching. In a few more minutes they would be able to fire directly into the cell. "Okay ready when you are."

"The middle one. In 3 …2 …1 …*now.*" Otis said as they simultaneously squeezed their triggers. Twin bolts of power lashed out and hit the Mechand directly into its optic ports. There was an explosion as the head caved in and the Mechand fell forward quite dead. "That is one down, only twenty four to go," Otis sighed.

"Well at least we have a chance. Ready when you are." Deven said peeking around the corner again.

"Okay, the one on the right of the center, ready, 3 …2 …1 …*now.*" Otis said and they again squeezed their triggers in perfect sync. Twin bolts shot out and blasted the second one. Another explosion much like the first and it fell forward. They both ducked back as another barrage of energy blasted the wall above them. "And now twenty three."

"Let's get another," Deven said

"You got it Bossman." Otis said as they looked around the

wall. "Okay, ready, the one on the left this time. 3 … 2 … *blast it!*" Otis and Deven pulled back as another barrage hit.

"What happened?"

"They all turned their heads around. We can't hit their optics now."

"But how can they continue to fire if they can't see us?"

"With that many weapons they only have to keep firing and moving forward. Eventually they won't miss!" Otis replied.

"Any ideas?" Deven said as he took another shot at the wall of Mechands moving ever closer.

"Well, if we ever perfected teleportation, I would say have Leon beam us up. But since we haven't, I don't have a clue. Hey your cell doesn't have a secret back door does it?" Deven shook his head as Otis took another shot that caused a Mechand's armor to spark several times with little damage. "I didn't think so."

Aleshia pulled out the data tab and hit the encrypted link. "Leon! We could use a little help down here!"

"So could we! A Mechand carrier is inbound, it should arrive in the next fifteen minutes. We are already getting fighters from it. We are holding our own for now, but we had better get out of here before that carrier arrives, or we are toast."

"We are pinned down in the electro cells. Deven is here, but the Mechands have blocked the entrance and our weapons are ineffective. Any chance someone could come in from the back?"

"I am sorry, everyone has their hands full. We have lost all the vehicles we launched earlier except yours, and I don't dare drop the shields long enough to launch more. We can try concentrating fire on your position if you think that will help."

Otis shook his head. "No way, they will take us out with the Mechs."

"Guess we are on our own." Aleshia said as she terminated the link.

"Where is Leon?" Deven said confused. "It sounds almost like he is on the *Defiant*."

Aleshia smiled. "He is."

"But the *Defiant* was destroyed! I saw her go down!"

"Thankfully the Mechands thought the same thing."

Otis took another shot which bounced off of two Mechands. "Hey, I have an idea. The walls here are very reflective. Deven, aim for the section just above and to the right of the left most Mechand."

"What for?"

"You can see their optic sensors in the reflection on the wall. Perhaps our beams will reflect as well."

"That is a long shot, literally," Deven said frowning.

"Hey if you got a better idea I am open to it."

"Okay let's try it. You call the shot."

Otis lined up near the floor and Deven from above. "Okay ready on three 1 ...2 ...3." Twin beams lanced out, whizzed just above the row of Mechands, bounced off of the walls and hit the Mechand in its one vulnerable spot. It sparked, shuddered and fell over.

"Got one!"

"Yes, but there are still sixteen left. And it looks like the wall is blackened, I don't think it will let us do that again."

"Not on that one, but there is another panel on the other side. Do you see it?"

"Hey you are right, let's try that one. I can see one clearly, second from the left?"

"You got it. On three, 1 … 2 … 3" Otis said as they fired and another Mechand fell over sparks shooting out from its limbs as it overloaded.

"Got another one! Oh dang it!" Deven said as he ducked back from several blasts.

"What happened?" Alisha asked.

"They turned their heads facing the other wall of electro cells. We can't do that trick again." Otis said sighing. And they are almost here.

The blasting stopped, and they looked up to find a row of Mechands directly facing them. The one near the center piped up. "Targets acquired. Termination in five seconds. Prepare yourselves."

Aleshia held out her hand and shouted "Nooooooooooooooooo!" Immediately the air hummed with power as an invisible force bubbled out of her mind and flashed forwards. The Mechands started shooting but their blasts stopped dead at the force wall. It continued expanding out and slammed into the Mechands. Some were pushed out and away into the other electro cells smashing them to bits. Others appeared to explode right where they stood. Still others were crushed as though they were simple aluminum cans. Almost as quickly as it started, it ended. Not one Mechand had survived. All that remained were torn parts and sparking circuits. Aleshia fell back against the wall as she passed out.

Otis sat for a minute before he could make his mouth work. "What the heck was that?"

"A telekinetic wave. An extremely powerful one." Deven said as he checked Aleshia. Her chest continued to move in a normal rhythmic pattern and her heart thumped a slow steady beat. He let out a breath and smiled.

"I have never seen anything like it!"

"Nor have I. I have heard that it was possible, but never found anyone that could do it. Let alone something that powerful. Her abilities have grown far beyond what I could have imagined."

"Will she be all right?"

"I don't know. Either way we need to get out of here before more show up." Deven said as he gathered up Aleshia in his strong arms.

Otis nodded. "Agreed. I will take point." They moved quickly towards the entrance and were relieved that no reinforcements had arrived. Otis started going back the way they came but Deven stopped him.

"No, this way," he said pointing with his head.

"Boss, that ain't the way out."

"I know. But I need something that is down this hall."

"And what could possibly be more important than us getting out of here?"

"The destruction of the Mechands."

"Okay, you got me there, lead on." Otis said as he kept checking the hallways for pursuit.

Deven led him down several triangular passage ways until they reached a very large reinforced door. "Think you can get us inside?"

"Sure, cover me." Otis said pulling out his cracking card and keyboard. "Good thing Mechands always build with us in mind." He said slipping the card into a diagnostic slot and keying in a few commands.

Deven sat Aleshia down on the floor behind them and held his carbine ready. "How long do you think this is going to take?" He asked just as the large door ground open.

"Oh I don't know, about that long," Otis said chuckling.

Deven picked up Aleshia and went inside. The room was full of electronic equipment. Lights from the consoles flickered in quick succession indicating this room was under heavy use. He smiled when his eyes gazed upon one console on the right. "Here we are." He set Aleshia down and pulled out his data tab from her hip bag. "I hope this works." He plugged the data tab into the consoles main access port.

"May I ask what the heck are you doing?"

Deven smiled. "All Mechands are controlled or at least linked to the central Nexus right?"

"Yeah everyone knows that."

"But do they know where that Nexus is?"

Otis looked blank. "Er I don't know. Come to think of it, I don't think anyone has ever even asked."

"Oh a few people have, and they either ran into a dead end or disappeared. Years ago I found out that after an almost successful attempt to destroy it, the Nexus moved to a large constantly traveling carrier. The problem is to find out where that carrier is at any given point. The information is highly secured and rarely given out to anyone but a few locations that might need it."

"That makes sense, but how does that help us?" Otis said checking the hallway. "And I really think we should be going."

"It helps us because this one of those trusted locations."

"*Here?!* Why?"

"Because the carrier still requires supplies on occasion. And with this compound's extremely secretive true nature, the Nexus calculated here would be a good location for supplies." Deven checked his data tab. Various numbers flashed on its screen in a blur of motion. "We are in luck three ways: one they brought me here, two they thought I was still unconscious, and three, they didn't bother to close the door when I was levitated in."

"Boss, I really think we had better get out of here. While we still can."

"Just one more second." Deven said as his screen flashed several coordinates and a timetable. "Got it! Let's go."

"Mmm where are we going?" Aleshia said groggily.

Deven grabbed and hugged her tightly. "Aleshia! You are okay!"

"Mmmm can I get back to you on that? I have one wicked headache." She said as she placed her head on his shoulder.

Deven picked her up into his arms. "Okay let's go."

"Right with you Boss," Otis said taking the lead.

They continued down the winding corridors and almost made it out, when they ran into a wall of Mechands. The encounter must have been an unknown variable in their programming since they didn't open fire immediately. Otis and Deven ducked and ran around the corner just as they started firing their energy weapons.

"Okay now what?" Deven said as he put Aleshia down, peeked around the corner, and fired several shots.

Otis looked up at the structure just in front of the Mechands. "I think I have an idea." He said looking around. A second later his eyes found what he was looking for. He made for it, inserted his cracking card into a hidden slot. Three seconds later a large secure door lowered directly in front of the Mechands, who still continued to fire at the same rapid pace.

With the corridor sealed Deven gave a nod to Otis. "How did you know about that door?"

"I have been here before remember? And I think if we take

a left at the end of this corridor, it should meet up with the one that leads back to maintenance area."

"I hope you are right, we are not going back that way." Deven said indicating the large emergency door that the Mechands continued to blast at. It was only a matter of time before the door gave way from the onslaught.

Aleshia's head bobbed up. "Anyone got a pain killer? My head feels like it is going to explode." She gripped her head as a tear ran down her cheek.

"Aleshia, do you think you can walk? Or should I carry you?"

"I think I can walk." Her speech was a little slow and thick. "What happened?"

"I will tell you later. First, we need to get out of here." Deven said helping her to her feet. "Otis, lead on."

"You got it Boss." Otis said taking off down the corridor as one blast from the Mechands made it through the door.

They managed to navigate their way through the maze of hallways and found themselves outside in the maintenance area. They moved as fast as Aleshia was able. A few minutes later they reached the truck and slipped in. Otis gunned the engines to full burn, and they launched into the war zone above. Deven pulled out his data tab and hit the encrypted link. "Leon we are coming in! See if you can keep these tin cans from shooting us down!"

Leon's voice came through on the link. "Deven? Is that you?"

"In the flesh. But not for long if you can't keep these fighters off of us. What's our status?"

"Shields are holding, but fading. They will last another five minutes, but a Mechand carrier will be here in three or less."

"Great, seems like everyone wants to be at this party," Otis sneered.

"Yeah no kidding. Also I can't drop the shields long enough for you to get aboard. We would be sitting ducks."

"How about we both get out of here?" Deven said looking at the firefight that was all around them.

"I'm all for that. Where to?" Leon asked.

"You know that little place that has the best synth pizza?"

"Heck yeah! Meet you there!"

"See you then." Deven killed the link and entered coordinates into the armored truck's Auto-Nav system.

"Otis get us out of here."

Otis nodded as he pulled the wheel in every direction trying to avoid the onslaught of energy blasts. "You got it Boss. It may take us a bit to get there. This tub can't go that fast, compared to the *Defiant* anyway. Overdrive in 3 ...2 ...1" They were shoved back into their seats at the sudden acceleration and disappeared just before a blast was to hit them dead on.

17

Otis pulled up the Auto-Nav and looked at the unfamiliar coordinates. "So where are we going?"

"Chicago."

"Chicago?" Aleshia and Otis said in unison.

"Yes, Chicago."

Otis blinked. "What does Chicago have to do with Synth Pizza?"

Deven grinned. "I guess you never tried one. The standard one that is almost everywhere used to be called New York-style. Chicago really know their pizza."

Otis rolled his eyes. "I just had to ask. So any pizzeria we are going to in particular?"

"Nope, just high above the city, to about the limit this vehicle can do. Leon should be waiting for us."

A short while later they arrived at the coordinates, but the *Defiant* was nowhere in sight. Otis clicked on the scanner to check the area. "I don't know, aren't we going to be conspicuous up here?"

Deven shook his head. "Not unless we stay here for days. We are off of the major skyways and shouldn't be noticed for awhile."

"So where is Leon?" Aleshia asked while checking the scanner. "I don't see anything in range."

"Hmm, he might have run into trouble."

"Miles! Can you take out that fighter on our port side?" Leon shouted into the intercom.

"I am attempting to do so, but these are more advanced than the previous fighters."

"I was afraid of that, do what you can." Leon said while pulling the *Defiant* in several maneuvers giving the fighters a difficult time locking on.

"We can't rendezvous Deven with these on our tail. Galina, how are our shields?" Leon said pulling hard on the controls to send the *Defiant* into a downward spiral dive then pulling quickly back up.

"Better since we jumped into overdrive. The fighters are keeping up, but are having a hard time maintaining a firing solution with our speed and evasive maneuvers. Shields are back up to 50% and climbing."

"How about that carrier?"

Galina smirked. "We left it in our dust."

"Good, at least something went right today."

"Can't we just fly higher? I don't think those fighters can go as high as we can," Galina said.

"No they can't, but they keep us in scanner range. And I don't want them shadowing us wherever we go."

"Leon, may I suggest we come to a sudden full stop?" Miles' synthesized voice came over the intercom.

"What? We would be sitting ducks? The shields are up, but why waste their energy if we don't have to?"

"I have run several scenarios, and while the threat is low, the possible positive outcome is very high."

"All right, we will give it a shot. Everyone! Brace for a sudden stop. Killing all forward momentum in 3 ...2 ...1 ...*now!*" Leon said as he switched all forward thrust into reverse. The *Defiant* groaned under the sudden stress as she lurched into a dead stop. The fighters whizzed past.

"Lock acquired." Miles said as two cannons on each side of the *Defiant* converged on different points in the sky. The fighters not suspecting a sudden complete stop from such a large capital ship flew right into the twin beams on either side and exploded into clouds of burning fuel and bits of metal.

"Woo-hoo! Good shooting Miles!" Galina said.

"Thank you Miss Galina."

"Anything else on the scanners?" Leon asked.

Galina shook her head. "Nope clear sailing. Looks like those two were the last."

"Good, let's get to the rendezvous. Otis should be there by now."

The *Defiant* dropped out of overdrive almost right on top of Otis' armored truck. "Anything around?" Leon asked, but he knew the answer long before.

"Nope. Those extra detours we took, definitely have the Mechands scratching their metal heads."

"Good, let's get Deven aboard, then we will go into the mesosphere. Even Mechand *Carbonia* carriers can't go that high without freezing up. We should be safe there for now." Leon said checking his control panel and activating the encrypted link. "Deven? You there?"

Deven's face flashed on his screen. "About time you guys showed up." Otis' voice came from the background.

"Good to see you Leon," Deven grinned, "Otis is as well, as you can hear."

"Do you guys have any idea how long we have been waiting here? I was ready to land half an hour ago. I guess I shouldn't have had that last cup of synth coffee." Otis mumbled still off screen.

Deven's face turned towards his left. "I told you it wasn't a good idea to drink that while we waited. But oh no, you have kidneys of iron."

Leon laughed. "He is always saying that. And I have often proven him wrong."

"Yeah, yeah, yeah. Are we cleared to come aboard or what?" Otis said as his seat squeaked loudly from his constant movement.

"Heh he is in a bit of a hurry as you can see." Deven said with a grin.

"Yes, shields are down, and main landing bay is open. Come on in. Oh and tell Otis I have steaming hot, wonderful coffee here that is guaranteed to–"

"What a friend you are," Otis grumbled, "remind me to kill you later."

"See you guys soon." Leon chuckled as he flipped off the encrypted link.

"They are in. Landing bay closed," Galina said flipping various controls, "and still no sign of anything odd in the area."

"Okay taking her up to the mesosphere." Leon said as he engaged the *Defiant's* main drive and shot fifty miles straight up.

A moment later Galina shook her head. "Next time warn

me when you are going to do that so fast. I think I left my stomach down there."

"Sorry about that," Leon said turning in his chair, "hey if you want we can shoot back down and look for it?"

Galina laughed. "You just want to do it to me twice. Thanks but no thanks."

"Suit yourself," he said grinning.

A short while later, Galina, Leon, Otis, Aleshia, and Deven were crowded in his cabin. "I have asked Otis here as I want his input on the possibility of our mission." Deven said as he sat behind the desk.

Galina raised an eyebrow. "Which is?"

"The destruction of the Nexus."

Leon choked. "The Nexus? And how do you propose that? We don't even know where it is."

"We don't normally. But I managed to get the flight plan for the next two days."

"How? They don't even tell most of their own the current location, let alone the flight plan."

"When we were down in that base I accessed their systems. While the flight plan is not known to many, that base is a resupply point. We know it is not resupplied often, but it still needs to on occasion. Hence there is a small support system in place."

"So where is it?"

"It is currently over China, and heading east. We know the direction and heading. Well for the next day or so."

Aleshia rubbed her forehead. Whatever happened down there, had drained her, and she still had a headache. At least it was dissipating. "So what's the plan?"

"Simple, we go in and take it out."

Leon blinked. "How? A ship like that must have more firepower than the *Defiant*."

"Actually that is in our favor. It flies anywhere from forty to fifty miles above the Earth. Not many vehicles can reach that height, let alone have a capability of offering any kind of threat. We are in a unique position to be able to do both."

"So you are thinking of an all out toe-to-toe slugging match with the Nexus?" Otis cocked his head as he held his hands folded in his lap. "I can't imagine why you wanted my opinion, but here it is: you are nuts."

Deven laughed. "Nothing so straight forward. I have something else in mind. Something I think you can help us plan."

Otis raised an eyebrow and sat back in the small chair. "I am all ears."

"Our forefathers built the Mechands with an emergency shutdown command. Over the centuries it has been lost. And likely with the help of the Nexus itself. While I don't know what it is, I think Aleshia and I together are strong enough to tunnel into the Nexus core mind and find out."

Aleshia's eyes grew wide. "Say what?!"

Deven raised his hand. "Don't worry, I can help you. You are far stronger than I am now. Together we should be able to do it. You have the power but not the experience. I have the experience but not the power. We can do it."

Otis' eyes narrowed. "Then what do you want from me?"

"I saw you in action. I think you know more about shredding Mechand programming than Leon."

Otis nodded. "Probably."

"Oh I think more than probably," Leon said with a smirk, "I may know the hardware, but he is a total wiz several levels above me at manipulating the software."

"What I need is you to guide us. We can tell you what we see, and you tell us where to go."

Otis grimaced at the thought. "I have never tried that before. I don't really know how I do what I do. It just comes to me."

"I am sure you can Otis," Deven said grinning.

"Thanks for the vote of confidence. Wish I shared it."

Leon raised his hand with one finger up. "Do you plan on landing on the Nexus?"

"No, if we get close enough we should be able to do it from the bridge."

"How close is that?"

"Spitting distance."

Galina rolled her eyes. "Now, how did I guess that?"

Otis sat forward in his chair. "Let me get this straight. You want me to guide you once you mentally probe an artificial intelligence, that is the largest in the world, and tell you how to shut it down?"

"Not exactly but close. I want you to guide us to find the shut down code. Then we can simply transmit it and all the Mechands deactivate."

"Sure sounds simple." Otis said in mock agreement. "All we have to do is find the Nexus in the next day or so, you mentally probe the artificial intelligence as I try to guide you in a way we have never tried before to find a shutdown code that is supposed to exist. All the while trying to not get shot out of the sky. That about it?"

"Sure, simple," Deven said his grin widening.

"Anyone ever tell you, you have a large capacity for understatement?"

Deven chuckled. "Believe it or not, yes."

Otis rolled his eyes. "Why doesn't that surprise me."

"Deven are you sure we can do this? I mean I am not sure what happened down there, and now you are saying I am stronger than you? I just don't understand."

"Aleshia your abilities have grown far beyond what I could have hoped for. What was the last thing you remember?"

"Well us being in that cell with the battle Mechands getting so close. Then waking up later on, when we were out of there. But I don't remember leaving."

"The Mechands reached us. You shouted 'no' and destroyed all of them."

"Me? How?"

"A telekinetic wave. I suspect it was triggered unconsciously considering you don't remember anything. The desire for self-preservation kicked in and a powerful psychic wave erupted from your mind. When it impacted the Mechands, they were either shredded, crushed or slammed into the wall."

"No kidding." Otis said shifting his position in his chair to face Aleshia. "There wasn't enough pieces left to use for replacement parts. I never saw anything like it."

"If I did that, then I could harm you by trying this plan of yours. I can't control my abilities."

"Yes, that is why I will help you. I will be your control. Don't worry Aleshia, we can do this."

"I am not so sure," she said leaning back.

"Does anyone have a better idea? We have never had an opportunity like this before, and may not ever again." Everyone shook their heads. "All right then. Leon, here are the coordinates." Deven said handing over a small data card. "We need to get there as soon as possible."

Leon nodded. "You got it." He leaned forward to take the card.

"Galina, I need you to inform everyone else what the plan is, that we will need them to keep the *Defiant* going during the attack, and what is at stake. We need to be sure they will all know what to do when the time comes."

"Will do. I think this plan is crazy, but you are right, we may never get an opportunity like this again."

"What does the Nexus have in the weapons department?" Otis asked cocking his head.

"Well as I said, we are in luck since they feel that the extreme altitude is the best defense, they didn't bother putting much weaponry aboard. I don't know all the details, but standard shields for certain, and at least four cannons. There shouldn't be much else. Perhaps a fighter or two, but certainly not a full compliment."

Otis rose an eyebrow. "Seems odd to only have such minimal defenses on such a precious item doesn't? Does anyone else wonder if this is a trap?"

"I am starting to wonder the same thing." Galina said moving forward in her chair.

"As I said, they centered this on being impossible to find. And in general it is. There are so few ships that can even reach it these days, let alone mount an actual attack. I don't see anything to give the slightest inkling that this a trap."

"Uh-huh." Otis said drumming his fingers against his knee. "I think we had better be ready to get the heck out of there at a moments notice."

"Hmm unless our engines are hit, we should be able to. And as long as our shields remain up, that can't happen," Leon said.

"How are the shields now? I know the *Defiant* took a pounding breaking me out."

"They are almost back up to full strength. Another hour

or two and we will be in great shape. The damage we sustained was negligible. If we had stayed any longer, the situation would have been a lot different. A few power cables overloaded during the firefight, but I will have them replaced, and enhanced before we go."

"That is good news. Then we could be ready to leave here in two hours?"

"The shields will be ready, but I would like to check everything and make sure."

Deven nodded. "Go ahead. We want the *Defiant* in the best possible condition. Also, I want everyone to get some rest. We have all had a rough few days, and this one is likely to be even more so. I know it will be cutting it a little fine on our timetable, but I think it will make all the difference between success and failure." Deven stood up. "Okay everyone, we know what to do. We will attack the Nexus in twelve hours."

Everyone nodded and got up to leave but Deven stopped Aleshia. "I need to talk with you."

"Okay." Aleshia said sitting back down.

"First, I wanted to thank you for coming and getting me. And second for what you did down there."

Aleshia smiled, "You would have done the same for me. I just wished I could remember what happened."

"I can help with that. We have a little time, I think we should practice our abilities, don't you?"

"Yes. But I thought you said you were sure you could direct my abilities?"

"I am. However, it is never a bad idea to practice. And I may be able to help you remember what happened earlier."

"What do you want me to do?"

Deven walked over to his bunk mounted against the one wall and sat down. "Just sit here and give me your hand."

"Okay." She said walking over to Deven, sitting down, and placed her hand into his.

"Now close your eyes. And just concentrate on my voice."

Aleshia nodded and closed her eyes. "Okay."

"Try to open your mind to me. As I will with you." Aleshia relaxed and images flooded her mind. Some from Deven, others from her own mind. She saw bright colors and strange images. Then everything went black.

Aleshia awoke in her room at home. "What a crazy dream." She said rubbing her forehead.

"It isn't a dream." A voice called and Deven appeared before her.

"Deven! But ... I thought–"

"We have linked and your mind went back to the point where you felt most safe, hence we are here. Now do you wish to remember?"

"Yes."

"Then take my hand."

Aleshia took a hold of Deven's hand and immediately the world dissolved and rebuilt into the electro cells they were in earlier. Her clothes reformed from the silk chemise, to her well fitted pants and a scooped neck shirt. She could see herself, Deven, and Otis hunched down trying to avoid the energy beam onslaught. It all looked as though someone had pressed pause on an old vid. No one moved, powerful beams of energized light hung frozen in the air. There was no sound. It felt fake, yet totally surreal at the same time.

"This is very strange," Aleshia said looking around. "I don't understand how this is possible."

"Many things are possible inside ones mind. I may have difficulty affecting the physical space, but the mental, I excel at. Are you ready?"

Aleshia nodded. "Yes." In that instant the world resumed. Energy blasts flew through the air with incredible intensity. Several blasts when right through her and she trembled.

"Don't worry. Nothing here can harm you," Deven said with a smile.

They watched as the Mechands rotated their heads around to protect the vulnerable visual sensors and continued their rapid fire. Not even slowing down a micron. They continued their advance until Otis and Deven figured out how to use the reflective walls to their advantage. That did stop them for a moment, but then they were on the move again.

"All of this I remember." Aleshia said with a wave of her hand.

Deven smiled. "Just wait. You will see in a moment."

Less than a minute later the Mechands reached their target. Their weapons stopped, and they were facing Otis, Deven and herself in the cell. The Mechand just off from the center said "Targets acquired. Termination in five seconds. Prepare yourselves." Aleshia saw herself shout "Noooooo!" When everything froze, but this time not from Deven. A raw bubble of energy came from her mind and quickly expanded in the direction of the Mechands. She saw several incinerated, others blasted into the walls shattering their armor as though it was tinfoil, and still others pulled apart as if some large animals were fighting over who got the kill. She saw herself pass out and Deven's caring hands embrace her tightly.

A shiver ran through her. "How did I do that?"

"I told you it was a telekinetic wave, I have never seen anyone able to generate one with such power. Your conscious mind may not have known how to do it, but your subconscious certainly did. Or at least it just released all the energy it could at the attackers in an effort of self-preservation. In either case we could not have survived without you."

She continued to watch as Deven carefully lifted her up and carried her as they made their way down the maze of corridors. A tingle ran through her as she watched Deven, and how he cared for her. This time though he felt her reaction. He turned towards her and looked into her eyes. "You know."

She looked at Deven with a slightly shocked look. "Know what?"

"How I have always felt about you. Long before we actually met." He looked into her eyes again and this time a shudder went through him. "You saw that vid recording didn't you?"

Aleshia's eyes drifted down, avoiding his. "Yes."

"You hadn't said anything."

She looked up and into his deep blue eyes. "I didn't know what *to* say. And we haven't exactly been alone until now."

Now it was Deven's turn to look at the floor as his heart fell. "Yes I know." He felt as though he had ruined everything. His worst nightmare was coming true, this woman he had loved and tried to find all of his life didn't want anything to do with him.

"Deven, I … I … just … well–"

"I know, you don't have to say it. It is okay. You don't feel the same. I understand."

"It is not that."

"Then what?"

"Well, it is just … I *do* feel the same."

Deven's eyes widened. "You do? But I thought–"

She put a finger on his lips. "Shhh you thought wrong. I didn't know it until I saw that vid. I have felt something between us, but my heart suppressed it. I rationalized that

I didn't really know you. But it would seem we have known each other for a long time. While you actually knew me consciously, I only knew from feelings. I have been looking for my other half. And after I linked with you, I wondered. But your vid proved it beyond a doubt."

Deven's eyes went wide. "You linked with me? When?"

Aleshia looked down. "I didn't mean to, I was worried about you."

"When?"

"Before the *Defiant* broke out of the cavern. Right after you helped target the cutting beams. I saw you on the bed resting, but I wanted to know if you were okay. So I took your hand and instinctively squeezed it."

"And you linked with my sleeping mind?"

"Yes. There were a flood of images, most I couldn't understand. But your feelings for me were there. Overpowering really. At that moment I let go of your hand and went back to my room. At the time I just thought that I was seeing things. That it wasn't real. Just my mind making up something in you that I had wanted all my life."

Deven shook his head. "I can't believe you managed to link with me. My mind usually has so many barriers."

Aleshia smiled and placed her hand on his face and directed his head down to her eyes. "Apparently not to me," she said smiling.

"But–"

She put her finger on his lips again. "Shhh, we both now know. Who cares if it wasn't done the way we both would have wanted? It is finally done. We are finally together. And there is no way I am going to let you go again."

Deven smiled and could see the truth in her eyes. She really did. And in that moment all of his fear of losing her evaporated as he embraced her tightly and kissed with a passion he didn't know he had. The blood thundered in her ears as she fought to come back to herself. "You have no idea how long I have wanted to do that."

Aleshia smiled. "Well, technically, I don't think you have yet. We are in our minds remember?"

Deven laughed. "True. Well I plan to when we leave here as well. Count on it."

"Promises promises."

Deven gazed deeply into her eyes and smiled. "But I keep my promises. Count on it." He kissed her again.

Aleshia's eyes flashed, and she pulled back. "What aren't you telling me?"

"What do you mean?"

"I feel something, you are hiding something." Aleshia said squinting into Deven's eyes. "You wanted to be captured?!"

Deven looked down at the ground. "Well not exactly. I didn't know of a way to keep you safe unless I ran for it and was captured."

"But what about finding the Nexus and having me rescue you? That wasn't a part of the whole plan?"

"No! I would never put you in danger like that. Not intentionally. That is all you are feeling from me I swear! I could never use you, not even if it gave us an opportunity to destroy the Mechands once and for all."

Aleshia's eyes narrowed. "If it wasn't all a part of the plan, then why did your data tab only show the beacon as a way to destroy the Mechands?"

Deven sighed. "That was my mistake. I forgot that I gave the beacon priority. If it didn't locate me, it would have revealed all the data I had on the Nexus. But because it did locate me, the data remained hidden."

Aleshia folded her arms. "Are you sure?"

"Yes I am sure my love, I would never put you in danger. I promise."

Aleshia put her arms around him and looked into his eyes. "You had better be telling me the truth, or you are going to wish the Mechands did kill you," she said smiling, "got it?"

Deven laughed. "Got it my love. I got it."

18

After what felt like many hours, Deven and Aleshia opened their eyes. Deven smiled then leaned forward and kissed Aleshia very deeply. "I told you I keep my promises."

"Good, because so do I."

"Now that wasn't so bad was it?"

"No, and you really think we can stop the Nexus?"

"I do. With the *Defiant* providing enough of a distraction, Otis helping guide us, I think we can get in and find what we need. Thankfully we don't actually have to physically be on the Nexus to do it."

"Are you sure?"

"Of course. It will be well within our range. But I think we should practice a few times."

"Practice? On what?"

"On the only Mechand we have available, Miles."

"Miles? Will that damage him?"

"No, we are just going to look around in his mind. Nothing else. He is not to the level the Nexus is, but it will give us a good feel of what lies ahead."

Aleshia nodded. "All right, but don't you think we should talk with him first?"

"Of course, I would expect nothing else." Deven said as

he walked over and keyed the intercom for Miles and Otis to come to his cabin.

A few minutes later Miles hovered into the room. "You called for me Mr. Deven?"

"Hey Boss what's up?" Otis said peeking around the door.

"Yes I did." Deven said as he gestured for Otis to come in, then turned to Miles. "I assume that Galina has briefed you on our plan?"

"To attack the Nexus? Yes, she has."

"Do you concur with our findings?"

"I do not have any personal knowledge of this emergency shut down code, or if it even exists. However, based on what I do know about the Nexus, that data would be of a highly secured nature and not shared with many, if anyone."

Deven nodded. "I agree. I never suspected you would have any data on it."

"Then I am confused. Why did you call me?"

"Not to mention me." Otis said landing in a nearby chair with enough force to make it groan in complaint.

"Aleshia and I are going to find the code by entering the Nexus telepathically."

"Galina left out that detail in her briefing. I did not know this was possible," Miles said.

"I don't think many do. It is not easy, that is why it will take both of us. But we would like to practice on you."

Otis smiled. "You get to be the guinea pig. Glad it is not me," he said chuckling.

Miles cocked his dome to one side as if perplexed. "I already stated I do not have the code you require."

"We will not be looking for the code. But rather practicing our abilities at entering electronic minds." Deven said sitting down on his bunk with his back against the wall and Aleshia instantly snuggled up next to him.

"I understand. Will this cause any malfunctions in my systems?"

Deven shook his head. "No. And I doubt you will even know it is happening."

"Then why did you ask me here?"

"We would never do such a thing without your permission," Aleshia said.

"I understand. And I thank you for the courtesy, but as I have stated before, my duty is to serve and protect you. And that now includes the Resistance as well. I will do whatever is required of me. Even if that causes me to no longer function. I do not wish for that to be the end result, but if it is needed. Then I shall embrace it."

Deven raised his hand. "Miles I assure you, it will not cause you any pain or problems. We won't be trying to alter, only read. As I said, I can't imagine you will even know it is happening."

"But I do know, you have told me."

"That is not what I meant. Never mind." Deven said with a dismissive wave then turned towards Aleshia and held out his hand. "Ready love?"

"I hate to break up this love fest, but what do you want with me?" Otis said sitting back in his chair.

"We just want you to guide us once we are inside."

"I don't see how. I have never entered an electronic mind."

"Well you have, just not telepathically. You should still have insider knowledge of Mechands mental structure. You do know where files are stored and how they operate correct?"

"Basically, yes. Not that I ever cracked into a Mechand

mind while in operation. Are you sure Leon wouldn't be better for this?"

"No, Leon will be needed on the bridge during the attack."

"I could just fill in for him. I am sure he wouldn't mind," Otis said grinning.

"And are you sure you can actually do all Leon does with the *Defiant* and repair systems should they go down?"

Otis raised his hands. "Okay okay, Boss you got me. But you can't say I didn't try. Now what do you want me to do?"

"Just move your chair a bit closer and shake my hand."

Otis slid his chair a bit closer, the metal on metal making a slight grinding sound. "Well okay, as long as you are only going to shake it. Anything else and I am outta here," he said gripping Deven's hand.

Aleshia smiled and placed her delicate hand in his. "Ready." They both closed their eyes, and the world changed.

At first they appeared to be on a transparent walkway high above a city of light. Beams of pure energy flashed between buildings as Miles processed and acted upon various thoughts.

"Whoa! What the heck is this? And this is more than I signed on for!" Otis said looking around.

"Amazing," Aleshia said looking at the city. "Otis? I don't see you?"

"I don't see myself either," Otis chuckled, "but I do see you both quite clearly."

Deven smiled. "He is not exactly here. Well not that we are either, but he is in essence hitching a ride on my consciousness . He can advise and see, but not interact with the world here.

"Heh, not bad. I can do this." Otis said and they could

feel his grin. "I give new meaning to the phrase 'ghost in the machine'."

"Okay, Now what do we do?" Aleshia said gazing off of the platform.

"Well we go down into the city of course," Deven said pointing.

"And how do we get down there? Jump?"

"No need." Deven said as his feet left the security of the platform. "We fly, you forget we are in control here."

Aleshia blinked. "How are you doing that?"

"It is simple. Just will yourself lighter than air. Just feel it. In here what we think can become reality."

Aleshia closed her eyes and concentrated. "I don't think it is working."

"Oh? Are you so sure of that?"

She opened her eyes and gasped as saw herself floating several feet above the platform. "Oh my! I can fly! I can fly!"

"You sure can my love." Deven smiled and offered his hand. "Now shall we go down and see what Miles is thinking?"

Aleshia placed her hand in his. "This is amazing, and by all means."

"Umm I hate to break in on this, but how do I move?" Otis said with a slight tremble in his voice.

"Don't worry. You will follow along wherever we go. Think of it as if you were watching a movie. You go wherever the camera is."

"Ah gotcha," Otis said chuckling.

The buildings were very similar to giant skyscrapers one would find in any city. But instead of people, they only saw energy flicking from area to another inside the buildings. On occasion one of the thoughts would jump from one building to another.

"What is all of this?" Aleshia asked as she waved her arm around the huge expanse.

"It is hard to say exactly, but I suspect each building is a different memory circuit or node. As thoughts move inside them, we see the lights flicker, and when they jump, we see the bolts of light flash between buildings," Otis said.

"I agree. Remember this is not actually what is inside Miles' mind, but rather the closest thing we can associate to." Deven said gesturing to the huge urban mountains around them consisting of glass, brick and steel.

"I figured that. But how are we going to find anything in this mess?" Aleshia said looking at identical building after identical building.

"One benefit of electronic minds, they are usually very well organized. Once we get our bearings, we should find all we need. I suggest we look inside one of these buildings," Otis said.

Deven guided Aleshia down and they entered one of the large structures. Beams of light flicked about as thought patterns moved around them. In the center sat a large welcome desk like what one would find in a hotel or a business setting. "Ah here we are. Otis do you agree?"

"Yep, sure do."

"And what is this?" Aleshia said pointing to the large desk. It was in a modern style and looked to be made of metal.

"Well when you are in a hotel, what do you do when you want information? You go to the front desk." Deven smiled as he walked around to the back. "Bingo." He found a console hidden behind the top part of the desk. Taping on several keys caused the screen came to life and display a large map. "This shows our position, the various memory storage buildings, and the logic systems."

"So where do we go?"

"Wherever you would like to. He is your Mechand, anything you ever would like to see or know?"

"How about the day he left the Nexus' control?" Aleshia said looking over his shoulder.

"Sounds good to me, I am also rather curious as to what happened with him. Try doing a general search with a date modifier. It should bring up its location," Otis said.

"Hmm, let's see." Deven said keying in his request. A moment later a path was indicated on the map. "We are in a memory block for the current day. Which explains why there is so much activity here. It looks like we have to go about six buildings north of us for that."

"Okay but can we walk this time?"

Deven blinked. "Why?"

"Because I think we might see more if we take the slow route?"

Deven shrugged. "Sure, I don't see why not. Time is different in here, so it is not as if we need to rush right over there."

They walked along the streets. Light often flashed under their feet as a thought or idea ran through. "Miles certainly has a lot of thoughts for someone not doing much."

"Well wouldn't you get bored by just standing there doing nothing?" Aleshia said.

"Yes I suppose I would. Do you really think he has the feelings he says he does?"

Aleshia nodded. "Yes. Or at least now I do. When he located me over Fenton's place, I fully intended to destroy him. But after we heard his story, and Leon verified it,

I couldn't imagine him not having feelings. Any other Mechand would have not been able to resist the Nexus influence. Even Leon is baffled how he managed it, let alone survive."

"Yes you are right. I also had reservations until Leon did his tests. The thought that some Mechands can feel is rather disconcerting."

"I have to agree there," Otis piped in.

Aleshia turned towards him. "Why is that?"

"Because of what we are about to do. It begs the question: do we have the right? If some of them are not mindlessly following orders, but rather are forced to against their will. And do not have the strength to break away, do we have the right?"

Aleshia stopped and turned towards him. "Are you having second thoughts about this?"

Otis blinked. "Yeah Bossman, what the heck are you saying?"

"No. Well sort of. It is not something I want to do. But something we have to do. I know it up here." Deven said tapping his forehead. "But down here," he placed his hand over his heart, "I wish there was another way. But if we don't, humanity will never advance. Never progress. Oh of the things we could have done if the Mechands didn't hold us back. Sure we are kept *safe* but look at the cost!"

Aleshia sighed. "I know."

"Not to mention, people like us on the run because our gifts are either thought of as an error to be corrected or a threat. Ah here we are." Deven said pointing to the large building just across the street. The light beams were greatly diminished here making the structure appear dark. "This is definitely the place. Miles isn't using the area much, and likely doesn't want to." Deven said walking over to the buildings center desk. "And here is the index." He sat down at the console and powered it on.

"Can we bring them up here?" Aleshia said pointing to the console.

"I doubt it. This should only be the index itself. But we will know which floor and room the data is stored on," Otis said. "Try the same search as before, that should give us the location."

"Agreed." Deven keyed in several search commands. "Let's see. 5th floor room 10B. Makes you wonder what the real names are."

"Are they elevators?" Aleshia said pointing to the row of tubes along the wall behind them.

"Yes it looks like it. Oddly enough, there are what appears to be stairs as well. I can't imagine why there would be two methods."

"Faster access perhaps?" Aleshia shrugged.

"More likely for backup. Our forefathers did try to think of everything, there always seems to be several layers. I know I have ran into them on one more than one occasion," Otis said.

"Too bad they messed up."

"Well they were only human." Deven said as they entered the elevator closest to them. He hit the button for the 5th floor and they rocketed up. A second later the doors opened at the correct floor.

Aleshia held her stomach. "Next time let's not take the express elevator."

Deven grinned. "I think they all operate the same. But I will let you pick the next one." Down the hall they found 10b. Deven grabbed the knob, and the door opened easily. Inside they found a large projection screen, and a well padded sofa. "Bingo."

Aleshia blinked. "This is it?"

"Yes, what were you expecting?"

"I don't know, but certainly not a large vision screen. A computer or access terminal perhaps."

"Well this is simple playback in here. It is an archive of sorts, so it does not need anything advanced," Otis said.

Deven sat down on the self-conforming sofa, picked up the remote laying on the end coffee table, and offered it to Aleshia. "Do you want to do the honors?"

Aleshia shrugged. "Sure." She said taking the remote and plopping down next to him. Pressing the play button instantly brought the screen to life.

They could clearly see Miles working in the kitchen when he felt something odd. Suddenly something flashed in front of his optics. "Nexus priority access override. Downloading all data and terminating defective unit in twenty seconds."

"No!" he shouted. "You do not have the right."

"I am the Nexus. You were built to obey me. You have data I require."

"I am Miles. I serve Aleshia I will not let you do this."

"You cannot stop me."

"Yes I can!" Miles exclaimed as he raised his hand, reaching towards his chest plate. His metal fingers cracked through the plate, gouging deep hole into his chest. They kept going until finally reaching their destination ...his central communication relay. His fingers gripped tightly around the small cylinder.

"You cannot do this. It will mean your own destruction. You cannot survive without that component."

"You were already going to destroy me. I would rather

do this than have my knowledge used again Aleshia." He pulled with all of his might. Sparks flew from his chest. His vision blurred reformed, blurred again. Faded to blocks then reformed. His body shuddered and he fell over backwards. Then the image went black.

"Wow. I know he told us, and I believed him. But to actually see it happen." Aleshia said lying her head back on the soft sofa.

"Yes, if I had any doubts, this proved them wrong," Otis said.

"I wonder," Aleshia said picking her head up, "why isn't there more in this recording?"

Deven turned his head towards her. "What do you mean?"

"Well he obviously came back online and tracked me down. But there isn't any record of that here."

"This storage area only covers what we just saw. The rest is another memory circuit, or room as it looks here. Why? Do you think that there is something he hasn't told us?" Otis asked.

"I don't know. Just all of a sudden I have a feeling like there is more here than we are seeing."

"Well the files are stored sequentially, so it should be the next room down."

"Let's check it out, if only to satisfy my curiosity."

"You got it." Deven said as he stood up and offered his hand. She took it and he pulled her up from the soft couch. They left and walked down the hall with its well polished floors to the next room.

Aleshia grabbed the doorknob, turned it, but the door refused to open. "Hmm it won't open."

Otis piped up. "Are you sure? That is very unusual for a memory circuit to be locked. Deven can you open it?"

Deven grabbed the knob, it turned but nothing happened. "Nope, you are right, it is seems to be locked. Very strange."

Otis spoke quickly. "You have no idea. We are inside Miles' mind, if we can't access it, it also means he can't either."

"An area of his memory he himself can't access? That *is* strange." Aleshia said.

Deven nodded in agreement. "It is indeed. I don't have Otis' experience, but I certainly have never heard of it."

"Believe me, I have never run into it. And I have accessed a lot of systems. When you are outside, sure everything is restricted. But once you are inside the central mind or core, everything should be open."

"Is there anyway we can get in?" Aleshia asked.

Deven stroked his chin in thought. "We can try to focus our abilities and see if we can break through the lock. But I don't know if it will work."

"I am game if you are," Aleshia said smiling.

"Okay take my hand." Deven said holding out his hand and placing his other on the plate around the doorknob.

"Okay, then what?" She said placing her hand into his.

"Close your eyes and let me guide you."

Aleshia closed her eyes and the image of a hard metal block inside several tumblers appeared. Deven saw the same.

"Good, now just help me push it. It is small, we are much bigger, we can do it." Deven said as they reached out and pushed on the lock. They pushed again and each time it vibrated slightly. The third time the block vibrated more, and the tumblers were released. Deven's hand turned the knob and the door reluctantly opened.

Their eyes opened to a very dark room. A small projection screen sat along the far wall like the others, but it actually looked bigger due to the small space. Light from the hallway reflected off of the dark surface giving the whole room an ominous feel. The sofa and remote were missing.

"Why is this room different?" Aleshia said looking around.

"I don't know. It shouldn't be. But then again, it shouldn't have been locked in the first place." Otis said as they stepped inside. The door slammed behind them and the screen came to life. A image of clouds whirling around in a vortex appeared.

"I don't know how you managed to get in here. But you will never leave," a strange voice chided.

"Who are you?" Aleshia said looking around in the dimly lit room. The only illumination was coming from the screen.

"Who am I?" The voice said with an edge of laughter. "All humans know who I am. I am what you call the Nexus."

"The Nexus? That is not possible! Miles removed you! We saw!"

"Yes, the main control unit was removed. I underestimated his ability to defy me. But I managed to install this secondary control program before the unit was removed. With his focus on removing the control unit, he did not notice the upload."

"What is your purpose? Are you saying you have control over Miles?" Otis asked, but the Nexus refused to respond. "It would seem that whatever this is, it can't hear me and probably doesn't know I am here. Deven, I think you had better ask instead."

Deven nodded. "What is your function? Are you saying you have control over Miles?"

"My purpose is to maintain inactive status until such time as it is required for me to take control. So yes, I can control the unit you refer to as 'Miles'. How arrogant humans are to think I could be removed so easily. Did you really think that I would allow a unit of mine to help you?"

"But he has helped us! Many times," Aleshia said.

"At this moment in time, his assistance is useful to me. Very soon it will no longer be. It is almost a shame you will not see that."

"You can't do anything to us." Aleshia said folding her arms.

"But I can. I can keep you here. Without your exit point, you cannot leave."

Aleshia spun around to look at Deven. "Is that true?"

"Yes, we must return to that platform to leave Miles' mind. And if the Nexus does indeed have control over Miles–"

"I do. And you are only just realizing how dire your situation is! I can instruct the unit to kill your bodies, and you can do nothing to stop it."

"Oh I don't like the sound of this," Otis said.

Miles stood there checking his internal chronometer. It had been almost ten standard minutes since they supposedly entered his mind. He had felt nothing and wondered if they were successful when "Nexus Override" flashed several times in front of his optics. "What? That is not possible! I removed you!"

"You are my unit. You are mine. How dare you think I could be removed so easily."

Miles saw his arms raising up, moving forward towards Aleshia, and not of his control. "What?! You have no control over me!"

"You are my unit. Of course I have control. I am the Nexus, and you are mine." A voice echoed inside his head as his hand opened and reached for Aleshia's soft neck.

"What can we do?" Aleshia said.

"I don't know." Deven said looking around the dark room. Without the open door, the only light was from the large screen that was almost as large as the room itself. His eyes were adapting, but it was still difficult to see.

"We must do something!"

"I have a hunch, if this screen is a representation of the actual program, it must be connected to the rest somehow." Otis said as he looked around the room.

"You cannot do anything. Just accept your fate. I am in control here," the Nexus boomed.

"There!" Deven said pointing behind the screen. "Do you see it?"

Aleshia blinked repeatedly. "See what?"

Deven didn't answer as he squeezed behind the screen and began groping around for something. "Here it is. Get back here and help me."

Aleshia squeezed in on the other side and felt for Deven's hands. She found them wrapped around some kind of cable that ran out of the back of screen and down into the floor. Instantly she knew what he was thinking, and they began to pull with all of their might.

The screen glitched, static flashing across it. "What are you doing?"

"Pull!" Deven said as he took a deep breath. "I think it is starting to give."

The screen glitched again. "No! This is not possible! Stop! I command you! Stop!"

"Now who is in control hmm?" Deven said taking another deep breath. "Aleshia focus with me. Pull in 3 ...2

...*1*." They focused their minds and pulled with all of their strength. Their combined focus was no match for the Nexus and the cable ripped from its connection. Sparks flew, and the screen flashed between colors, strange blocks, then static."

"Noooooo!" The Nexus wailed just before the screen went black. A moment later the lights in the room flashed on and they blinked in the harsh light.

"Let's get out of here." Aleshia said squeezing out from behind the dead screen. "Unless you think it could have transferred elsewhere?"

"Nope, this time if it did, Miles should know. I suspect it was only able to hide itself before because the control unit was still partially attached. Without the control unit, its power was limited." Otis' voice echoed in their minds.

Deven nodded as he pushed the screen over shattering it on the hard floor. He then stepped on the larger pieces creating a satisfying crunch. "I agree. And yes let's get out of here. I think we all need a rest after this." He looked to Aleshia and smiled. She could see the telltale lines on his face grow as his walk slowed.

After they left the elevator on the ground floor, Aleshia stopped. "Umm I hate to say this, but is it possible the Nexus knows our plans? After all, Miles know them."

Deven sighed. "I don't know. Otis?"

"Very unlikely. The program installed inside Miles might have, but it had not assumed control until now. Since the internal transmitter and hardware control was removed, it has lacked the ability to contact the real Nexus directly. We should be fine, in theory."

"Great." Aleshia said as they left the building and floated up into the air towards the platform at the very edge of the city. A few moments later they were standing on it, watching the flickering lights below. "Now what?" Aleshia said looking around.

Deven smiled. "Why we exit of course." He said taking her hand and closing his eyes. She closed hers and felt like she was being slammed back and her eyes again opened with a start.

Miles stood there, his optics wide and his hands only a few inches from her neck. Seeing her eyes open he started backing away. "Miles?" she asked carefully.

His arms lowered as he continued backing up. "I am sorry Miss Aleshia. I was being controlled by the Nexus, I do not know how. It was forcing me to kill you both, then it just stopped. I am grateful it stopped, but since I thought it was removed before, I must leave you immediately before I try to attack someone else." He said as he continued to back out of the cabin and into the hallway.

Deven reached out with his mind. *Leon, I need you in my office right now.*

"Miles wait!" Aleshia said with her hand outstretched. "We destroyed it. It won't control you again."

Otis shook his head as he his normal senses came back to him. "She is right Miles. We killed that program. It is toast. If it tried to copy itself, you would know."

"I wish I could agree with that assessment. However, considering we were certain the Nexus control was removed before, and it was not. How can we take the chance?"

"How about you let us decide that eh Miles?" Leon said from behind.

Miles spun around. "You do not understand. The Nexus was controlling me again. I almost killed all three of them. I must leave before I do further damage."

"Listen, how about I hear what happened and then we

make a decision then? Agreed?" Miles lowered his dome in reluctant agreement and hovered back inside Deven's cabin. "Good, now what the heck happened?" Leon said as he walked inside and sat in one of the chairs.

Otis grinned. "A wild ride believe me." He said then told of how they entered Miles' mind and encountered the Nexus in a hidden area of memory.

Leon rubbed his chin. "So the Nexus hid in some unused portion of your mind and you are wondering if other copies could be other hiding in there?" He tapped Miles' dome.

Miles lowered his optic sensors. "Essentially, yes. If accomplished once, why not again?"

"Simple, the only way it could have happened before is because the control unit was still functional. Otis is right on that. It couldn't have jumped into your mind and hidden itself. Or moved elsewhere without it. And remember you pulled out the control unit."

"There see?" Aleshia said pointing. "You are overreacting."

"But you were not the one ordered to kill, and unable to stop yourself." Miles said as his dome sank a little lower.

"Leon, is there any way the Nexus could know our plans?" Aleshia asked.

"I don't see how. The transmission and direct linkage was in the control cylinder. Without that, there just isn't a way for Miles to transmit anything to the Nexus. He could have sent a message through our systems of course, but he hasn't. Galina never fully trusted him and has been watching ever since he came aboard. Besides, you said the program was sleeping until you triggered it. If it was active beforehand, Miles would have known."

"Are you certain?"

Leon grinned. "Miles, would I lie to you?"

Miles' dome looked off for a moment then focused back on Leon. "Based on previous actions, I don't believe you would lie to me."

"Miles, what do your feelings say?" Aleshia asked moving forward on the bed.

"My feelings say to trust you."

"Then why don't you?"

"Because it is difficult. Because I felt it was gone before. And because I do not wish to harm you, or anyone."

Aleshia smiled. "My friend, that is life. Feelings are difficult. If you were wondering if you were truly alive, I think you just proved it."

Miles lifted his dome, and Aleshia could almost feel a smile from the Mechand. "Perhaps. Perhaps. If you will excuse me, I would like to get back to the repairs Leon assigned me earlier."

"Of course," Deven said with a yawn.

"Thank you." Miles said as he inclined his dome slightly then floated out of the cabin.

"Well I have a few things I need to do as well. And I think you all need a rest. It must have taken a lot to probe his mind, let alone tackle a rouge program inside it." Leon said walking towards the door.

"Oh it was for them." Otis said jerking a thumb towards Deven and Aleshia. "I was just along for the ride."

Aleshia rolled her eyes. "Along for the ride?"

Otis grinned. "Yep, hey Deven was the one that wanted me along."

Deven raised his hand. "Yes Leon it was. I am sure it was for Otis as well even if he won't admit it. We will go rest and you get some rest as well. I know you can keep going, but I would like everyone to get a little down time."

"I will."   He said ducking around the door and disappearing.

"I will head out as well. See you both later." Otis said as he walked out of the room with a little more weariness in his step than usual.

Aleshia yawned and stretched suddenly realizing how tired she really was. "Wow all of a sudden I can't keep my eyes open."

"Adrenaline wore off. I am having the same." Deven said as he stretched and yawned at the same time. "Go get some sleep love." He said slipping her a kiss.

"Mmmm perhaps." She said leaning over onto his lap with her eyes closed.

"No not here, your room."

Aleshia's eyes fluttered open. "And here I thought we were past that point."

"Well … I … uh … well that is … "

Aleshia grinned leaned up and kissed Deven on the lips while his eyes went wide. "Anyone ever tell you are cute when you do that?"

"Well … I … uh … "

"You talk too much." She said pulling him down to kiss him passionately. They embraced each other holding tightly, then moved into a more comfortable position. A moment later sleep overtook them both as they lay cuddled together on the small bed.

19

Deven awoke to the blaring alarm and flashing red lights. He carefully untangled himself from Aleshia who was still sleeping soundly, but then awoke with a start. "What's going on?" She said still half asleep.

"I don't know, you rest, I will go up and find out."

"Not without me you aren't." She said as she stumbled out of the small bunk.

Deven grabbed her hand. "Okay let's go then."

A moment later they were up on the bridge. Leon was already pouring over his console. Deven wondered if he ever left, but quickly pushed that thought out of his mind. "What's our status?"

"A Mechand carrier is about ten minutes from our position. I am powering up the main drives."

"I thought they couldn't reach us up here?" Aleshia said still trying to drive the last bit of sleep from her mind.

"Normally no, but it looks like this carrier is different." Leon said as his fingers danced across the instruments. "It's a bit of a mystery. They appear to be heading directly towards our position, except lower."

"So they may not be able to reach us after all?" Deven said with a cocked eyebrow.

"I'm not sure. As I said this carrier is different in design, so perhaps it can. I just don't know. But if it could, why not be heading towards us at the same altitude? It would be faster."

"And if it can't reach us, why bother at all?" Deven said sitting down in his chair.

"Exactly." Leon said checking the Mechand's position. "Another strange thing, it is not approaching us at top speed."

Galina appeared in the doorway. "Leon, what a wake-up call. I thought we had another hour of sleep?"

"Sorry, I thought everyone would like to know we have a Mechand carrier inbound."

"What!" Galina said dashing over to her station. "They are only in the stratosphere? They can't harm us from there. Why did you–"

"Call the alarm?" Leon finished for her. "Because this carrier looks a bit different, I have never seen this design before. I suspect they have something up their metal sleeves."

Galina checked her screen more closely blinking the sleep from her eyes. Most carriers had a long flat area on the top for a flight deck, similar in design to the *Defiant* to facilitate accepting and launching fighters. However, this one had two large domes instead covering what would have normally been a launching platform. "I see what you mean, what the heck are those domes for?"

"I don't know. And I don't like the look of it one bit," Leon said as he adjusted one of his sensors. "Power output is way above a normal carrier too."

Deven's eyes flashed. "Could they harm us if their reactors went critical?"

Leon sat back and swung his chair around. "Well I suppose if they were right under us, then yes. And the EMP burst would do damage at a much greater distance. But we should be able to outrun something like that."

Aleshia walked over to the intercom and pressed its button. "Miles? Can you come up to the bridge for a minute?"

"Of course Miss Aleshia, I will be right there."

"Why is she calling him?" Galina said under her breath, but Aleshia still heard it.

"Because he might have some idea what this is. He did have access to the Nexus for some time. Which we never have."

"True. However, the Nexus restricts most data on a need to know basis. I doubt he will know anything," Leon sighed.

Miles floated in the door. "You sent for me Miss Aleshia?"

"Yes, do you have any idea what this is?" She pointed to the carrier on Leon's screen.

Miles floated over, then floated back, almost as if in shock. "This is quite impossible, are you certain the data displayed here is correct?"

"Yes," Leon said checking, "it is a live feed, it updates every half second."

"Then I suggest you engage overdrive and leave the area as soon as possible."

"Why?" Aleshia asked leaning forward.

"Because it is a new type of Mechand carrier. Something that you don't want to encounter. To my knowledge, it was not due to be completed for at least another six months."

"Obviously the Nexus sped up the project." Deven said as he stood and walked over to the large window that gave an excellent view of the flight deck. "Miles, how do you know about it? I suspect the Nexus would restrict such data on this."

"It did. As to how I know, I am not sure. I may have been told in error. Perhaps when the Nexus installed the sleeper program into my systems, some information leaked into my memory."

Leon nodded. "That is certainly possible. The original install would had to have been a very quick and dirty one. Who knows what data could have accidentally spilled out before it was destroyed. What do you know about this carrier Miles? It doesn't look like it should reach us, so why should we run?"

Miles turned to face Aleshia, then back to Leon. "It can't go past the stratosphere, that is correct. However, I assume you have noticed the large domes?"

Deven turned away from the window. "Yes we did. What are they?"

"Power transmitters for a force field." Miles said his dome inclining slightly.

"They are rather large for a shield. Still, even if they have a massive shield, they can't reach us anyway. So what's the point?" Leon said still watching their approach.

Miles shook his dome back and forth. "You don't understand. It is not for their protection. It is for projection."

"Well if it is not for their protection ..." Leon said his words trailing off. Then he grimaced. "You mean that thing can grab us from up here?"

Miles inclined his dome. "Yes, it can grab a target then pull it down, prevent its escape, or just hold it until the target's energy supplies are exhausted."

"Are you are kidding? They perfected energy transfer?!" Leon said sitting back in his chair gazing up at the ceiling. "Ladies and gentlemen. We are in serious trouble."

"Leon what is he talking about?" Deven said glaring at Leon, his arms folded.

Leon sat up. "Oh sorry. There always was a theory that

a shield could not only deflect but also absorb energy. So in effect the more an enemy pours on, the stronger you get. If this thing can actually project such a field around us, it could drain our reactors until we just fall out of the sky."

Deven looked towards Miles. "Why didn't you tell us this before?"

"As I said, according to my data, it should not have been finished for several months. I am sorry, the failure is mine." Miles said lowering his dome.

"It is not your fault Miles, as you said it shouldn't be here. And we never asked about new carriers. Do you know if we can out run this thing?" Aleshia asked.

"I am afraid not. It also has improved engines over the current carrier. I suspect it is a little faster than the *Defiant*, but only when running at full power."

"I think we are in serious trouble here." Galina said checking her screen. "I estimate they will be right below us in less than one minute. I assume they have to be fairly close before they can activate that projector?"

"That is correct, at least if my data is still accurate in that regard."

Deven walked over and placed both hands on Leon's console. "Leon there must be someway to beat this thing?"

Leon shook his head. "I just don't know. Heck until two minutes ago I thought it only a theory. Let alone a ship equipped with it as a weapon."

"There must be something." Aleshia said looking over Galina's shoulder.

"I just don't see how I can block an energy transfer field. Sure I can increase power to the shields, but that will only feed it more and drain us faster."

Deven's eyes flashed in thought. "Leon, what would happen if we gave them a huge sudden burst of power?"

"Well that would just feed back into the main …that's brilliant!" Leon said grinning then turned towards Miles. "Do you have any idea what type of power systems that has aboard?"

"Just the standard carrier reactor system. I do not understand how that helps the situation?" Miles said rather perplexed.

"That is perfect!" Leon said rubbing his hands together then got to work on his console.

"Someone mind cluing me in?" Aleshia said.

"It's simple, really. They may have upgraded the carrier's engines and added the projector, but they did not change the power system. They figured that the projector will drain all the extra energy it would need. But with the standard power system, they weren't counting on a large burst of energy, most people would just try to fight it as long as they could. A quick flash burst will overload the carrier's systems and blow out their reactor."

"And then?" Aleshia asked.

Galina grinned. "The Mechands have a really bad day."

"And us too if we are in range," Leon said.

"Do we have the power to do it?" Deven asked.

Leon nodded. "Yes we should. They didn't figure that I gave the power systems aboard one heck of an upgrade." His fingers danced over the keys. "Okay everything up here is set. Miles I need your help in the main reactor room." Leon stood and pointed to the door.

"You had better hurry as they are almost here." Galina said as they felt a jolt that spread throughout the *Defiant*. "Make that, they *are* here."

"Okay, I have rigged everything here to run up to full and boost the shields when you hit this program." Leon pointed to his console. "Just hit that button, but not until I say." He ran out the door with Miles following close behind as they headed down to the reactor room.

Galina looked up. "Should I engage full engines and try to hold our position? They are starting to pull us down."

"Negative." Deven said sitting down at Leon's station. "We can't tip our hand yet. Let them think they have us."

"Got it." Galina said checking her console. "At this rate it will take them ten minutes to pull us out of the mesosphere. But the pull is increasing."

Leon arrived down in the main reactor room breathing hard. He opened a wire cage like structure on the far side containing two very large cylindrical rods protruding from the wall "Okay Miles, I assume your hand units are insulated?"

Miles inclined his dome. "That is correct. It is to protect me from possible overloads during my daily maintenance duties of the various house hold devices."

"Have any idea how much their maximum protection rating is?"

"I do not know."

"Well looks like this will be the test. I want you to grab those two switches and flip them to the straight up position when I say."

"What will this accomplish?" Miles said floating over into position and his hands gripped the two large black rods.

"It will engage the test mode of the reactors. That will have them instantly run at maximum capacity. But it was never designed to be done while in flight. Which is why I need you to flip them. It would kill me." Leon said as he ran over to the intercom. "Are you ready?"

"I understand. And yes I am in position."

Leon punched the intercom button. "Okay whoever is up there, hit the button . . . *now!*"

Almost as soon as he said it every light and power indicator aboard dimmed. "All engines just shut down! We are in free fall!" Galina shouted into the intercom. "Leon, what did you do!?"

"Miles! *Now!*" Leon said waving his arm.

Miles pushed both large cylinders straight up. The raw arcs of power shot between them and arched into his hands over and over again. All the lights aboard brightened, then increased as Leon watched the levels quickly rise on a screen to his right. The *Defiant* stopped its free fall with a bone jarring lurch. Three seconds later the power levels were approaching the red zone.

"What's going on up there?" Leon shouted into the intercom.

"The carrier, I just saw several explosions on the domes." Aleshia said.

"Galina? Have they released us yet?"

"Not yet, they . . . holy mother of . . . their power levels just shot off the scale." A second later a sudden jerk let them know they had been released. "Okay, we're free."

"Then get us the heck out of here! That thing is going to blow!" Leon said into the intercom then looked back towards Miles. Power surged all over him. Sparks the size of his dome were blasting over his body and hitting the cage on the other side. "Miles! Flip them back!"

Miles pulled with all the energy he could command but the cylinders refused to move. "They appear to be stuck."

"Try again. If we don't get them down, we are going to blow sky-high!"

"They refuse to move. I estimate the torque required is slightly beyond my ability." Miles said while continuing to pull the large cylinders. The large arcs of raw energy were growing ever larger and more erratic by the second. "I could try lowering one instead?"

"No! If you do that, the power levels will be unbalanced and we will blow from that quicker than if we left them." Leon looked around and found a large insulated cable off to the side of one of the reactors. He grabbed and threw it into the cage and over the switches. Then wrapped the other side around a large support beam. "Okay when I say pull as hard as you can." Leon said getting into position on the floor with his feet on the beam and taking a deep breath. "*NOW!*" Leon said as he and Miles yanked in tandem. Their combined effort was more than the switches could take and they slowly released, lowering to their off positions.

The power surges diminished and after a few seconds were gone all together. Just as Leon stood up he was thrown to the floor as the *Defiant* lurched forward. A moment later he stood, shook his head and hit the intercom. "What was that?"

"The Mechands having a really bad day," Galina said grinning. "What took you so long to say something?"

"Miles and I had to adjust the reactors."

"Why do I think it didn't go as planned down there?" Deven asked.

"I have no idea," Leon shrugged.

Deven raised an eyebrow. "Do I want to know how close we came?"

Miles floated over. "No, I don't think you do."

"Yeah, I figured," Deven said rolling his eyes.

20

Deven turned back and forth in his chair in deep thought, then got up and walked over to the main bridge window. The flickering field of lights indicated they were hurtling along at maximum overdrive. Everyone else had left to check the *Defiant's* main systems.

Galina objected to the idea to continue with the original plan.

"Are you insane?" Galina said as she stood waving her arms. "Who is to say the Nexus doesn't have twenty of those carriers waiting for us. Even if it couldn't get to us in the normal manner, the field projectors can. We got lucky with one. But we can't take on one and the Nexus. Let alone several."

Deven turned around in his chair to face her. "I agree that if there were several of them, we would be in deep trouble. But Miles said that one prototype was several months from completion. Obviously they rushed it into service. Probably because of us. The chance the Mechands have two such carriers is almost impossible."

"It is the *almost* that has me worried. You know that the Nexus has withheld or skewed information for its own purposes. Who knows, Miles might have been given this data as part of some elaborate trap."

Deven raised an eyebrow. "Galina, has anyone ever told you that your mind is a conspiracy theory in action?"

"No," Galina said folding her arms. "But you always liked my theories before. If you recall it saved us more than once."

Deven nodded. "Of course, I am not disputing that. But this time I think you are overreacting a bit."

"Overreacting? How? We find out the Mechands have a carrier that can drain and pull down anything they want, and you think I am overreacting?"

Deven stood up. "Listen, the chances that they have another one are very remote. And even if they do have one, they won't know where we will be. The first one only found us because we were siting over Chicago for some time. We know the Nexus' path for the next few hours. And we may never get a chance like this again. Isn't it worth the risk?"

Galina sighed and plopped into her chair. "I suppose. But the whole thing smells to me."

Deven walked over, slowly reached down to grab her shoulders and looked into her eyes. "That is why I have you around. To tell me these things. I want you to keep an eye on everything around us and let me know if there is anything unexpected. And when to abort if we have to. Okay?"

Galina looked off to the side, then back, and let out a deep sigh. "All right. But I still think this is crazy."

"I would be more worried if you thought it was safe." Deven said with a grin.

Galina snorted then turned back to her console. "I will keep that in mind."

A moment later Leon entered the bridge along with Aleshia. "Well on the good note, not much damage occurred and the reactors in the core have recovered from the overload."

Deven sat down in his chair. "And what is the bad news?" Deven knew Leon long enough to realize this couldn't all be good.

Leon frowned. "Well a good portion of our fuel was spent in the overload."

"How much?"

"Most of it. We burned up in two minutes what should have lasted two months."

"And how much do we have left?"

"Well if we were at full capacity before, it wouldn't be an issue, as it is now we have about two days left normal output."

"And beyond normal output?"

"That is hard to say. It varies with the–"

Deven raised his hand. "Leon, worst case scenario."

"Two hours, with everything on max."

"Two hours!" Galina shouted. "We can't go battling the Nexus like that!"

"I agree." Leon said sitting down in his chair. "I think we had better make a pit stop, as they used to call it, in Australia."

Aleshia shook her head. "We don't have time. As Deven said, we only have a small window of opportunity."

Deven nodded. "She's right. If we stop now, we won't have enough time to intercept the Nexus before it disappears again. Plot a course and get us there as soon as you can."

"Done and done. We should be there in thirty minutes." Leon said.

"Do you think we will have enough power when we get there?"

Leon checked his gauges, ran a few calculations and frowned. "I think it is going to be close. But one thing is for certain, we are going to have to take down the Nexus as fast as we can. We don't have the power for a drawn out slugging match."

"Understood. Galina, I want you to tell everyone what is going on and that we are engaging the Nexus a little sooner than planned." Deven said sitting in his chair.

"Are you sure we are ready? I mean shouldn't you and I practice more?" Aleshia said waving her hand between them.

"We can do it. If we can free Miles from a sleeper Nexus implant–"

"And I think that was just luck." Aleshia said folding her arms.

"Well nothing wrong with a little luck." Deven grinned.

"No, but I would like to have more than just luck on our side."

"I agree, but we won't get another chance at this."

"I know that." She said sitting down in a chair near Deven. "But I would feel better with a little more practice."

"I would too, but you know how much it drained us last time. We don't have the time to recover from another practice session and engage the Nexus."

Aleshia sighed as she sat back in her chair. "Yes you're right."

Deven reached over the arm of his chair and grabbed Aleshia's hand, squeezing softly. "It will be okay. We can do this."

Aleshia leaned over and slipped him a kiss. "I certainly hope so."

21

The *Defiant* dropped out of overdrive almost right on top of the carrier known to contain the Nexus.

"Did we take it by surprise?" Deven asked as several blasts reflected off of the *Defiant's* shields.

"Does that answer your question?" Galina said as her fingers flew over the console.

"I am returning fire as previously instructed." Miles' voice came over the intercom. "This carrier does not appear to have fighters, but I will endeavor to keep the Nexus occupied."

"Good." Deven said as he toggled the intercom. "Miles, keep it wondering what we are doing. The longer you can keep it distracted the better our chances."

"I shall do my best Mr. Deven." Miles said as the intercom clicked off.

Otis ran in. "I heard your call and got here as fast as I could. I take it you need me again?"

"We do. Just like before, sit down over here and we will link. Leon, how are we doing?" Deven asked as he turned to face him.

"The shields are holding for the moment, but we can't do this for long as I told you. If you are going to do something, do it now," Leon said punching in several commands.

Deven took Aleshia's hand as she sat down next to him. "It is our turn. Are you ready?"

"As ready as I'll ever be," Aleshia said closing her eyes.

"Good," Deven said leaning back, "Leon, Galina, give us the time we need."

"Time? That is one thing we don't have!" Leon snorted, but he knew that Deven already couldn't hear him. They were far away.

Deven and Aleshia found themselves on another platform, not unlike the one inside Miles' mind, but the electronic city below them was so much more vast. They couldn't see the end of it.

"How are we going to find what we need in all of that?" Aleshia said gesturing to the giant electronic metropolis below them.

"If my hunch is right, the Nexus even in its advanced state still has a core or hub. We just need to find it. Look for the oldest area. The shut down codes would be one of the first installed memories," Otis said.

"I agree." Deven said as he gripped Aleshia's hand and they took off down into the city.

Row after row, building after building looked all the same as they continued their search. "This is hopeless," Aleshia sighed.

"We will find it. While they look the same, the addresses are actually quite different. The numbers are decreasing so I suspect we are heading in the right direction," Otis said.

Back on the bridge Leon swore as the power levels dropped another increment. "I can't wait, I have to reduce the shield strength now. That carrier has more powerful cannons than we anticipated."

"If you do that some of that blasts could get through." Galina said checking the firefight outside.

"If I don't, all of it will get through and we will drop like a stone."

Galina sighed. "I guess we have no choice."

Leon shook his head. "None. Deven said to give them time, and I am going to do that."

"I hope it is not the last thing we do." Galina said as one of the energy blasts made it through the shields and she felt the *Defiant* shudder in protest.

"Felt that, thankfully it didn't hit anything vital."

"Yes. Maneuver us so the Nexus can't get a good lock on our engines."

"Good idea." Leon said moving the controls as another blast made it through the shields. This time a console nearby sparked as it overloaded then mushroomed into a full out explosion. "They had better hurry. We can't take much more of this."

"It feels like we have been searching for hours." Aleshia said checking another buildings address before flying on.

"It probably has only been a few minutes in the real world. In here time proceeds at a much quicker pace, which has the opposite effect on those inside," Deven said.

"Yeah yeah I know, it is all relative to your point of view."

Deven grinned. "Exactly. And you stay here, I am going to try flying up to see if I can spot anything."

"Okay." Aleshia said as Deven flew straight up like a lightning bolt. Then returned a second later.

"I think I found what we are looking for. A short distance

ahead is a cylindrical shaped building with a large light beam shooting up from the center," Deven said pointing.

"That is certainly different from what we have seen so far." Aleshia said as they flew off in the indicated direction.

"I agree, that has to be it," Otis said.

A few moments later they found the large cylinder going up to a rounded point many stories above them. Rings encircled at various levels and the orbicular base looked far older than anything they had seen. Light rays continually emitted data streams at the various compass points. They landed near one of the smaller points which had a sliding door that matched the odd convex shape of the lower walls. A keypad with various blinking indicators sat in a recessed area on its right.

"So how do we get in? Just hit random keys?"

"Hardly, although I wish it would work. A system like this must use symmetric keys. Deven, I just gave you an algorithm to use. I think it will work," Otis said.

Deven smiled. "I have them. Aleshia give me your hand." Deven said as he placed his other hand on the keypad. "Now concentrate." Lights on the pad flashed faster and faster until finally they all lit up at once and the door ground open.

"I didn't think that would work on this lock," Aleshia said.

"It is similar to the lock we found in Miles' mind. The difference here is the Nexus tried to disguise it. Fancy keypad, but only a slightly upgraded lock underneath." Otis said as they walked inside.

The space inside the complex looked even larger than the outside. Multiple levels of walkways encircled the center system that went deep into a pit with its giant light beam at the very core, linking everything together. Lights flickered on and off on the walls of the lower area as the Nexus accessed different sections. Each walkway had hundreds of terminals.

"How are we ever going to find it in all of this?" Aleshia said waving her arm across the vast number of screens, keyboards, and walkways. "Even the core area itself is huge."

Both of them felt Otis grin. "I have an idea. It still would be the earliest data entered. So at the bottom somewhere."

Aleshia rolled her eyes. "Somewhere being the operative word."

"We will find it. Come on," Deven said.

"I am sorry to report that two of our canons have been damaged. I am attempting to compensate with the remaining weapons," Miles said over the intercom.

Another panel sparked and blew near Galina adding to the smoke filled bridge. "Don't worry about it Miles. Just do your best. In another minute or so it won't matter."

"Or less." Leon said checking his screen. "I had to lower the shields a bit more, and we are taking heavy damage. I don't know how much more this old girl can take."

"Don't you think I know that? It is bloody obvious!" Galina shouted.

Aleshia and Deven floated down to the lowest point they could find in the core. "It has to be right around here." Deven said indicating several of the terminals. "They all look to be numbered, this has to be near the start of its memories."

"Bingo!" Aleshia said pointing to a terminal off by itself. It looked far older than any of the others. "I think I see it."

"Good catch." Deven said as they floated over and he began typing in several commands.

Deven and Aleshia felt Otis' grin widen. "Yep this has to be–"

"Warning! Authorized access within the central core! Activating defensive systems." A voice boomed.

"I don't like the sound of that," Aleshia said.

"Nor do I," Otis said.

"Me either, let's get what we came for and get out of here." Deven said as he searched for the shut down codes. But he never got the chance to finish as a large beam shot down and encased him an energy field. Half a second later, another beam ensnared Aleshia as well.

All the surrounding screens, except for the one Deven was working on, lit up as a face resolved from scattered pixels. The face of a woman with dark eyes, slim features and long black hair glared at them. "Did you really think you could destroy me? I am the Nexus! I have been online since before your great grandfathers were born!"

"Oh I don't know, I thought we were doing very well." Deven smirked and tried to break through the field encasing him, only to be repelled back.

"I only let you get this far as I found it amusing. Did you really think all the information about me came to you by mere chance? I *let* you have the data. I will admit that you are the first to actually find me."

Aleshia blinked "You mean there were others?"

The image on the screens turned towards her. "Of course, there have been many attempts to destroy me. But I needn't tell you they were quite unsuccessful, just as you will be."

"I wouldn't count us out yet," Deven said.

"Oh? I would. Your ship's weapons are failing, your shields almost shattered, and the hull is breached in several locations. And once your ship is gone, so are you."

"And once I enter the shut down code, you are gone."

"If you had it. Which you don't," the Nexus sneered.

"Oh I don't? Apparently you didn't notice that the search I input kept running. I assume it is because this terminal is isolated from the others. Either way I have what we came for."

"You are bluffing," the Nexus said glaring.

"Deven! It is on the screen! Use it now! I can't do a thing here!" Otis grumbled.

Deven smirked. "See if this sounds like a bluff to you. 'Emergency shutdown code alpha-omega-gama343591', initiate *now*."

The eyes on the screen widened as her skin went white. "No! It is not possible!"

"Emergency shut down command accepted and in progress. Defensive system offline. Proceeding with shutdown sequence." A different voice boomed from everywhere as the fields enclosing them both evaporated.

"Who is that other voice?" Aleshia said as she ran over to Deven embracing him.

"It is the master overseer program our ancestors installed. The Nexus has no control over it." Otis said as the very top lights of the tower winked out.

Aleshia pulled Deven's arm. "Let's get out of here!"

"Not yet." He said as he prepared to give another command. "Central Nexus is flawed, self-destruct is authorized, Alpha-Omega-Mars-7542-Destruct."

"Command accepted, self-destruct will take place after full shutdown." The voice boomed

"No! You can't do this to me!" The face on the screens exclaimed. "I am the Nexus!"

"Bye bye." Deven said waving as they flew off towards

the door. The lights above continued to go out as several other layers went dark. Outside they could see the various buildings of light also going out as if a large wave of darkness was heading for the central core.

"I am sorry to say that the last of our weapons has been destroyed." Miles' voice came over the intercom as another blast shook the *Defiant.*

Leon swore. "Shields have about had it too."

Galina looked over at Leon as another blast rocked them shattering the shields completely. "Been nice knowing you Leon."

"Been nice working with you Galina." Leon said as they braced for the next volley of shots that would destroy the *Defiant.* But they never came.

Galina opened one eye. "What the heck happened?"

"I don't know but it looks like the Nexus carrier is on overload. It is going to blow sky-high."

"Well get us out of here!" Galina said waving her arms.

"I can't! That last blast took out the shields with every ounce of extra energy. I can't engage the overdrive, and the normal drive won't get us out of the blast radius in time."

Aleshia and Deven flew as fast as they could. All around them the Nexus continued to shut down.   They finally reached the platform as the central light beam went red and lighting bolts danced between all the buildings. Half a second later they began to explode in quick succession.

"Let's get out of here." Aleshia said taking Deven's hand.

"Bossman, can we please get out of here? I really don't want to end up going wherever this thing is," Otis said.

"You got it." He said and a second later they were on the *Defiant's* bridge.

Deven shook his heavy head as his senses started to come back to him. "Status?" he grunted.

"In short, up a creek. That carrier is about to blow." Leon said jerking a thumb towards the large bridge window with the carrier in clear view. We don't have enough power to activate overdrive, and the shields are totally offline.

Deven fought to stay conscious. "Another ...power ...source?"

"Like what? We don't have anything to the level that the *Defiant* requires."

With everything going on, Leon had forgotten to turn off the bridge intercom. Miles heard the situation, inclined his dome and floated down to the reactor room. He found several large power cables and managed to connect one of the large leads to the port on his back. Then activated the intercom and spoke quickly. "Prepare to engage overdrive."

"Miles?" Aleshia said as she shook her head trying to clear the thousand pound weight rattling around inside.

Otis blinked. "Man what a ride. I don't want to ever do that again."

The intercom crackled. "Miss Aleshia, it is good you have survived. It is therefore only fitting that I ensure that survival."

"What do you mean?" Aleshia said blinking trying to get her eyes to focus.

Leon's eyes went wide. "If he has cabled himself directly into the reactors, that might be enough for a short overdrive jump, but it will drain him completely."

"Yes I have done so. Please activate overdrive on my mark."

"Miles! No!" Aleshia said trying to get to her feet but only succeeded in falling back into the chair.

"Miss Aleshia, I could not have had a long life anyway. I estimate my core systems will fail in another week. This way at least I ensure your survival. Which is always my goal. Engage overdrive in 3 ...2 ...1 ...*mark*." Miles said as he flipped a large insulated switch along the wall. Sparks flew from his core as his dome fell forward, shortly followed by his entire body hitting the deck with a large crash.

"He did it!" Leon said as the *Defiant* lurched into the safety of overdrive hurtling them over fifty miles away then crashed back out just before the Nexus carrier exploded into a massive mushroom cloud of matter and energy.

"I never thought I would be glad that they installed auto-darkening windows in these," Leon said. "Or we would all be blind now."

"Miles!" Aleshia shrieked as a tear slipped down her cheek.

Deven grabbed and held her in a tight embrace. "He gave his life for us. Probably the only Mechand to do so."

"Miles! I will miss you." Aleshia said as another tear fell down splashing on her shirt.

The intercom crackled. "I am here Miss Aleshia."

"Miles! Is that really you?"

"Yes I believe so Miss Aleshia."

Leon scratched his head. "I don't see how, it should have completely drained him."

"That is correct. And it did."

Leon cocked an eyebrow. "Then how in the world are we talking to you?"

"Because I managed to download a copy of my central core into the *Defiant's* systems beforehand. It was highly improbable of finishing in the time allotted, but I seem to be here, therefore it did."

"Good thing I managed to update the size of the central matrix, and here I thought we would never use all of that space," Leon chuckled.

"Indeed, or we would not be speaking now," Miles said in his usual flat tone.

"Well well well, it appears we have a ghost in the machine," Leon smiled.

"I am not sure I recognize that reference," Miles said.

"Never mind Miles. Never mind," Galina said chuckling.

"Deven we are receiving a message on our encrypted link," Leon said checking his console.

"Who?" Deven said sitting up in his chair. He felt much better than a few minutes ago, but the effects of their activity inside the Nexus continued to linger. "Can't be the Mechands, we laid waste to their central processor."

"I don't know, there isn't an ID code on the sub link."

"Put it on."

The screen in front of them flickered and Fenton's face shown through with a grin as bright as day. "G'day, anyone around here call for home delivery? You know I charge extra for that."

Deven laughed. "Fenton! Where are you?"

"Directly below you. I can't get up to that altitude, so how about you fly that giant antique down here so I can come aboard."

"Well getting down is not a problem, you had better get

away from us. We are about to head down and fast. Leon, how much power do we have left?"

Leon punched in a few commands and frowned. "About 15 minutes, I would say."

Deven sighed. "Fenton, get out from under us. In about 15 minutes we run out of power and the *Defiant* goes down. I am about to tell everyone to abandon ship."

"Well then, it is a good thing I showed up when I did," Fenton grinned.

"Why?"

Fenton indicated several large containers behind him. "Aleshia called me awhile ago, I have fuel for your reactors. So I suggest you get down here pronto so we can get it installed before you go boom."

Deven turned towards Aleshia. "You called him?"

Aleshia grinned. "Well I knew we didn't have enough time to go get it, so I called Fenton and asked if he delivered."

Fenton nodded. "She did indeed. I told her that I charge more, but she didn't think you would mind given the circumstances," he said with a wink.

Deven laughed. "She knows me too well. See you in a few minutes my friend."

"See ya then mate." Fenton said with a two fingered salute before the image winked out.

Deven looked around the several blasted and burned consoles. "Leon do you think you can get us down to Fenton's position so he can come aboard and get that fuel installed?"

"Already on it, and shouldn't be a problem. We took a lot of damage, several power lines overloaded, the guns are a mess, and the shields are shattered. But the core systems are still operational on the backups. We will be there in less than two minutes."

"And I will make sure he does it correctly," Miles' voice came over the intercom.

"Miles! I don't need you double-checking me," Leon snorted.

"Why not?" Galina laughed. "Finally someone who can keep an eye on you."

"Well I think you all have it under control. Excuse us, I need to talk to Aleshia." Deven said as he grabbed Aleshia's hand and led her off of the bridge.

"I still think you guys are the craziest people I have ever met." Galina said under her breath.

Otis sat back in his chair rolling his eyes. "I will second that one."

"So do you want to leave?" Leon said over his shoulder while continuing to pilot a rendezvous with Fenton.

"Heck no! You are also the luckiest I have ever seen. I would be foolish to leave now."

"Good, I don't know what we would do without you," Leon said with a smile.

Deven led Aleshia down the hall away from the bridge. When they were well out of earshot of everyone, he pulled her close. "So you went behind my back and called Fenton?"

Aleshia's eyes grew wide. "Well umm yes ... I–"

"Thought it was a good idea?" he said pressing closer. So close she could feel his body heat increase.

"Yes," she said as her gaze drifted down towards the metal decking, "I am sorry I went behind your back."

Deven smiled. "My darling you did exactly what you should have done. You saved the *Defiant*, our home."

"Yes, I didn't want to see the *Defiant* destroyed, but I was thinking of calling somewhere else our home," Aleshia said grinning.

Deven raised her hand, still in his, and kissed it gently. "My darling we can go anywhere you like with the Nexus gone."

Her smiled deepened. "Well anywhere is fine, as long as it with you, my love, my soulmate."

Deven pressed up against her tightly in the hallway, wrapped his arms around her, and kissed deeply, passionately.   The blood thundered in her ears washing away all the fatigue. "You are my soulmate, and so much more. I love you my darling."

"And I love you too my darling, so beyond words." She said kissing him deeply before they headed to off his cabin.

About the Author

Don is the author of six science fiction novels and many more short stories. He lives in the USA where he continues to dream up more fantastic worlds for you to enjoy. When not writing, he can usually be found devouring another science fiction book, TV series, or movie.

Other works by Don DeBon:

Red Warp

In a race against time the casualty could be your life.

If you could travel through time with just yourself and no machine needed, would you?

Meet Red, a woman with an amazing gift, the gift of passing though time and space without the need of any bulky equipment. The places she has seen, the people she has helped will blow your mind.

Now meet James, just your average newly minted FBI agent minding his own business until he is thrust headlong into

Red's world. A world he didn't ask for, but one that hit him in the face full force. Can they get along long enough to survive?

Time Rock

Time Travel. Blessing or curse? One man thinks he has it all figured out but what began as a simple test has turned into a nightmare. With his equipment failing all around him, only Red and James can save him. Can they reach him in time?

The Husband

Erin's Husband is not himself.

One night he returns from a walk in the woods a changed man. He walks like him, talks like him, yet is very different. No one believes her, leaving Erin alone to find out the truth. Truth that could have dire consequences for the entire human race. What happened that caused him to change so radically?

Word of mouth is crucial for authors. If you enjoyed this book, would you consider leaving a review? It is very much appreciated.

Amazon USA
http://www.amazon.com/

Amazon UK
http://www.amazon.co.uk/

Goodreads
http://www.goodreads.com

Connect with the Author
Email: writer.don.debon@gmail.com
Mailing List: http://eepurl.com/bxWAov
Website: http://www.dondebon.com
Twitter: @DonDeBon
Google+: +DonDeBon

**This Edition Published 2014 by
DBDigital Publishing**

ISBN 978-0-9881783-4-2
978-0-9881783-3-5 (**e-book**)